"53 Days"

"53 Days"

a novel by

GEORGES PEREC

edited by Harry Mathews & Jacques Roubaud

translated from the French by David Bellos

VERBA MUNDI
David R. Godine · Publisher

BOSTON

First published in 2000 by
DAVID R. GODINE, PUBLISHER, INC.

website: www.godine.com
Copyright © 1989 by Editions P.O.L.
Translation copyright © 1992 by HarperCollinsPublishers

Originally published in French as "*53 jours*" by Editions P.O.L., Paris,
in 1989. This translation first published in Great Britain by
The Harvill Press, London, in 1992.

Library of Congress Cataloging-in-Publication Data
Perec, Georges, 1936–1982.
[53 jours. English]
53 days : Georges Perec ; translated from the French by David Bellos ; edited by
Harry Mathews and Jacques Roubaud.
p.   cm.

I. Bellos, David. II. Mathews, Harry
III. Roubaud, Jacques. IV. Title.
PQ2676.E67A1613   1999   98-33645
843'.914–DC21   CIP

ISBN   978-1-56792-545-6

Fourth Printing, 2020

This book was printed on acid-free paper
in the United States of America.

CONTENTS

I

53 DAYS

CHAPTER ONE

15 May

The army and the police are still patrolling the city.

Ten days ago, for the twentieth anniversary of Independence, the miners of Cularo held a rally in Avenue de la Présidence-à-Vie which left eight dead, amongst them a woman and a child. A state of emergency was declared, bringing in its wake a string of irritations and constraints. The alleged ringleaders were arrested, all gatherings were banned, cars were searched, and a six p.m. curfew was imposed. Obviously, like all other schools, the Lycée Français was closed.

Grianta began to seem all day long what it normally was only from noon until five – a dead city, crushed beneath its heat and its own silence. It was really very curious, in the late afternoon, at the hour when crowds ritually flood beneath the colonnade of Place de la Paix, to see the café terraces practically empty – waiters standing in lines, stock still, behind the potted azaleas, holding big circular trays under their arms, gazing blindly at the few soldiers seated behind their half-pints of fizzy orange. A week ago, the chief waiter at the Brasserie de Paris was roughed up for having spilled zabaglione on a second lieutenant in the Flying Squad, since when the waiters of Grianta have put up unbeatably effective passive resistance to the whole officer corps. With all the appearance of impeccable zeal, they manage to take a good twenty-five minutes to serve a lemonade or a *granité*.

I have hardly been out at all these last ten days. I just take a little turn around the town centre every evening between five and a quarter to six, mainly to hear the birds. At that hour, they flock in their thousands in the eucalyptus trees, but there is usually such a crowd that you can hardly hear them. I take the opportunity to buy some supplies before going back in. Gino's has closed, in order to avoid the four or five raids the police would not fail to make every day. With the curfew, in any case, most of his regulars do as I do – they stay in. It's not much of a life. French newspapers are banned, and there is nothing to watch on television apart from the golden smile of the President-for-Life and his imposing lady-wife's numerous jewels beneath her equally numerous chins. What with the audiences he grants, the speeches he delivers, the nurseries she opens and the receptions they attend, the two of them fill a full forty minutes of the evening news hour, the remainder being devoted, in decreasing order of screen-time, to the Minister of the Interior ("the man on the up"), police announcements, meetings of the Agricultural Reform Commission, football (the national sport), the evening's "cultural slot" (the orphans of the Monférine Girls Home making flower garlands for the visit of the President-for-Life, the finals of the International Folk Dance Competition at the Ministry of Handicrafts and Tourism), and the forecast, of unrelieved, oppressive tropicality.

At first I was not displeased to have nothing to do – I mean, nothing in particular. It made a break in the usual routine which at this time of year often begins to seem if not absolutely unbearable then at least very burdensome – lessons to prepare, scripts to mark, parents' evenings. So it was like having holidays imposed seven weeks ahead of the long-hoped-for "real" ones. I had a fair bit of reading to do, including a thing on labyrinths by Rosenstiehl, a few whodunits, and a collection of crosswords which had only just arrived from Paris. But I am not displeased now – quite the contrary, in fact – to be entrusted with a specific task. It's something new for me, and therefore quite exciting.

This morning, the Consul called me on the telephone. He wanted to see me as soon as possible, and summoned me to lunch with him at the bar of the Hilton, which is considered here to be one of the heights of style.

I got to the hotel at five to twelve. The appointment was for noon (I am almost pathologically apprehensive about being early, or late). I wore my light grey alpaca suit and a tie, which aroused noisy hilarity from the bunch of guards kicking their heels in front of the Institute of Archaeology. I didn't take offence. You must be mad to go out in Grianta half an hour before noon wearing a suit and tie, and I had dithered for hours before deciding that I should dress correctly for the occasion even if it meant being quite wrongly clad for the climate.

Two submachine-gunners stood guard in front of the Hilton entrance. An uncommonly corpulent NCO in camouflaged battle-dress patted me all over to make sure I was not carrying a weapon. Past the revolving door, seated at one of those little desks with blotting pads habitually placed in the lobbies of grand hotels for guests wishing to deal with their correspondence, another soldier asked for my passport, leafed through it maddeningly slowly, then threw it onto his blotter. Condescendingly, he gave me to understand that the passport would be returned to me when I left the hotel.

There was no one in the bar. No customer, no barman, no waiter. The air-conditioning and the semidarkness made it appreciably cool. The piped music was smoothly and cleverly anodyne (an arrangement for a big string band of an old hit called, if my memory serves me right, "Il pleut sur le lac de Côme," or something like that) and sufficiently low in volume not to impinge very much.

I sank into a blood-red leather wing chair with a perfect patina, and began to wait. I didn't dare clap my hands for service, as is the custom in all the city's other bars and cafés. I looked around and tried to recall on what occasions I had been here before. With Beatrix? With Lescale? With the Feders? Certainly not often, and only at the start of my stay here, for very soon my personal tastes led me to prefer the deck-chairs of the café terraces in Place du 5 Mai, or the wisteria-laden bowers of the Italian ice-cream parlors in Avenue de France. In any case, I recalled very well having previously observed the consummate skill of the Hilton's interior decorator, who, by combining obligatory cosmopolitanism, the requisite elitism and a no less statutory measure of local colour, had respected the canons of contemporary taste to a tee: there were a few shimmering reproductions of apocryphal mariners' charts enlivened to very slight excess with AFRIQYA INCOGNITAs and hairy-maned monsters, which hinted at the ancient mirage of explorers bold; the stuffed white shark, the gazelle's horns, rhinoceros head, elephant tusks and giant tortoise shells brought an exalting whiff of big game and deep-sea fishing to overstressed executives; whilst the genuine sharkskin upholstery of the arm-chairs, the mahogany of the bar, the brass inlaid all over the place, the Tiffany-style lampshades and the authentically tartan fitted carpet gave reassurance that the great traditions of Western com-fort had been wholly and scrupulously respected, and that the Customer would be treated here as the Very Important Person that he or she could not now fail to be. As for the crafts of the locality, they were modestly but meaningfully represented by four large ochre-daubed urns, a few masks, scimitars and pan-gas, and tall, narrow raffia hangings decorated with geometrical arabesques which formed a flimsy screen between the bar proper and the dining lounge.

Towards ten past twelve, a waiter in black pantaloons and an embroidered red spencer appeared. I asked for a beer, which he brought me almost straight away, together with an assortment of olives and savouries. The Consul had still not come. Perhaps it was his custom to be late?

I hardly knew him. Like all other French residents of Grianta, I received twice-yearly invitations to very formal consular garden parties, but I had in fact attended only one, the previous year, on Bastille Day, when I exchanged no more than a couple of polite-ness with the Consul. I saw the man again at greater length on three occasions in January, when he asked me to man the French Book stand at the Grianta Exhibition and Fair – a job which wore me out, which was almost entirely useless in enhancing the cul-tural standing of *la patrie*, but which got me the perk of a trip back to Paris on expenses. What I knew about the Consul was what everyone knew: he had served in a small Italian town before tak-ing up his post in Grianta about ten years ago, was a *bon vivant* (in his own estimation), a discriminating eater and a knowledgeable drinker, played tennis rather well and bridge rather badly (I'm the exact opposite), and collected minerals. He sometimes went on brief expeditions into the desert to collect fine specimens. He was about my age (forty-something), came from Rouen without being of Norman stock, had just failed to get into a *grande école*, and admitted to regretting it. Stories were told about his private life because his wife – a tall, rather gloomy blonde – spent more than two thirds of the year in Bordeaux, where their two children were at college. However, not one of the formidable gossips of Grianta (where the principal form of social life in the French colony, I hardly need say, consists of retailing rumour, calumny and idle chatter) has ever come up with any evidence of the Consul's theoretical flings. The most commonly touted view was that he kept a mistress in a villa near the Golf Club (the smartest part of town, where ministers have their residences), but if he really does, then he does it with such discretion that nothing of it has ever actually transpired . As for his politics, they were of more than diplomatic evenhandedness. In private, he posed as a liberal, disapproved of the police-state methods of the President-for-Life, understood the trade unionists and the students who were trying to do something about it; but in the exercise of his official capacities, his utter caution was not far short of plain cowardice. On one occasion, a year before I got here, and before the local (official and parallel) authorities had lifted a finger, he forced a university lecturer to flee to France for having read his students an article from *Rouge*. He justified his action retrospectively, saying he had wanted to spare the man the torture and imprisonment he would otherwise have had to endure before his inevitable expulsion.

Whilst I sipped my over-chilled beer (refrigerating drinks is a local custom to which I have never taken), several waiters emerged. They began to lay the tables for the "DeLuxe Snack" which customers in a hurry would soon come to eat, and then they brought in trays of appetizing hors d'oeuvres and desserts. I was beginning to get hungry and impatient.

The Consul turned up at twelve thirty-five. He seemed quite surprised to learn that I had been waiting for forty minutes and asserted abruptly that he had told me half-past twelve. He took exception to my drinking beer, even imported beer – "Didn't you know that they have to add some stuff to it to stop it going off?"

and bluntly ordered two White Feathers. Usually I can't manage whisky, but this one, heavily diluted with fizzy water, turned out to be perfectly drinkable and refreshing. We chatted about this and that for a few minutes. I gathered that he wasn't particularly eager to talk about the political situation and I prudently avoided making any allusions to it. A maître d'hôtel came to take our lunch orders. I allowed the Consul to choose rolled baked burbot with papaya for me, a far less exotic dish in Grianta than the veal cutlet with spinach that he ordered for himself. He studied the wine list at length, sniffing quizzically several times as he read, and settled on a bottle of chilled Lambrusco. I was surprised at his unpatriotic choice.

"Good French wines and true," he replied, "are not what they should be when they get here. Few travel well, and the cellars here are either sweltering, or abominably refrigerated. It's true we could have had a Hermitage, but it might be rather heavy; and we should have had it uncorked earlier, and even decanted . . . "

We rose to select our hors d'oeuvres from a side-table, and came back to our seats to nibble. Then the Consul came to the point.

"Has Serval been to see you?"

I raised my eyes from my plate and stared at the Consul with astonishment.

"Serval? Robert Serval."

"That's right, the very same."

Like all French residents in Grianta, I had heard of Robert Serval. He is one of our national treasures in these parts, so to speak. He writes whodunits which quite often still sell three hundred thousand copies in France. He came to live here a few years ago and occupies a suite on the top floor of the El Ghazâl (at 125 piastres a night!). He is hardly ever seen out. The few people who have had occasion to approach him describe him as an eccentric misanthrope. Crozet, who has read two or three of his books, says that they're not badly put together, but a bit fuzzy on the details. As for me, despite being quite a fan of detective fiction – mainly by English writers, to tell the truth – I have never wanted to read or thought of buying a Serval.

"Why would he have come to see me? I don't know him!"

"But he knows you, so it seems. You were at school together."

I was struck dumb.

"Serval? I never had a friend at school called Serval!"

"Of course you didn't! That's only his pen name. Didn't you know? His real name is Réal, Stéphane Réal."

I shook my head again.

"That name doesn't mean anything to me either."

The Consul seemed surprised and almost irritated.

"It'll come back to you. In any case, his memory could hardly be clearer. You were both at the Collège d'Etampes, in second or third form, in the early fifties. It seems you even sat next to each other in class, where you had a teacher called Lemarquis. From what Serval told me, I gather he was a real horror."

"I was at Etampes, that's right enough, in third form, in 1950, and I've not forgotten that old idiot Lemarquis one bit. But Réal? Stéphane Réal?"

The Consul looked at his watch.

"Listen, I've not got a lot of time. I'm leaving on the Paris flight at seven, and I've still got a lot to sort before I go. But I must bring you up to date on the situation."

He stopped talking for a moment whilst our table was cleared.

"Serval disappeared last Wednesday. He was playing poker in his room, with three partners. Gambling was one of his few passions, did you know that? Apparently he has lost his shirt at cards more than once in his life."

"But gambling is forbidden in Grianta," I observed.

"That is precisely one of the things that brought him here. He had got himself banned from most casinos in Europe, but the temptation was still too strong over there. All he could do here was to play poker in private, for stakes which were usually no higher than a couple of thousand dollars.

"In short, he was in the middle of playing a game when someone rang him on the telephone. He went to his bedroom to take the call. According to the three other people present at the time, the conversation lasted barely thirty seconds. He came back to the main room, and told his partners to carry on without him, or to take a break until he came back. He said, literally, that he had to go out for ten minutes at the most. He went to the hotel garage and asked the night watchman to get his car out, whilst he went to parley with the duty guard. We have since learned that he was given a safe-conduct valid for thirty minutes, for the purpose of getting himself to the French Embassy.

"It turns out that one of the card-players was none other than Charlier, the manager of the El Ghazâl. An hour later, he rang the concierge, who confirmed that Serval had indeed left the hotel in his own car. Charlier then had the duty guard put on the line; a little later, they contacted the Embassy staff, who told them that no one there had either rung Serval that night or summoned him to the Embassy.

"As you might expect, no one told me anything until two days later. Meanwhile, Serval's red Jaguar was found abandoned in a car park in Rue d'Alzire. The police investigated, and the Embassy did so too. I double-checked everything they found, which came to just about nothing: Serval caught no plane, boarded no boat, took no train. Since the events, everything that moves here is under such tight control that you can be sure it's true. Besides, no ransom demand has been made known. Investigations continue, officially. Which means that they're looking down a few wells, trawling the lagoon, and that every few days a couple of sidekicks from the CID and the Embassy meet to deliver make-believe progress reports to each other. In actual fact, they're not onto anything at all, and I would be amazed if they ever came up with a lead.

"I must tell you that this whole affair bothers me a great deal, and for a reason which you will appreciate easily. Serval was aware of being under threat, and he took steps to let me know. The first time, about three weeks ago, he asked me to lunch at the El Ghazâl. The invitation astounded me, coming from him, for he had made it obvious ever since he came here four years ago that he intended to give his compatriots as wide a berth as possible.

"It was over that lunch that he mentioned you. He told me he had recognized you when he saw your name and photograph in *En Avant!*, in the article about the launch of your book stand. Had you come over from France especially for the exhibition? Or were you resident here? He seemed glad to learn that you taught at the

Lycée Français, and promised to get in touch with you again as soon as he could. Then he added:

"'I didn't bring you here just to make sure it was my old school friend. What I'm about to say may seem fantastical or puerile– but I do believe that I am in danger.'

"My face must have expressed stupefaction, because he then fell into an almost embarrassed silence. I didn't know what to say. I ended up asking a stupid question: had he received threatening letters?

"'No, that's not it. Look, I can't tell you what's been going on. Perhaps it's all just groundless suspicions, or a set of coincidences. I hope to be able to reassure you in a few days' time, but if it is what I fear, then I will need your help, at very short notice, and I wanted to warn you in advance.'

"That was all I could get out of him at that first meeting, and lunch came to an end without another mention of the unspecified danger.

"I waited several days for Serval to contact me again and ended up calling his hotel myself, out of sheer impatience, but could not get through to him. Finally he got in touch with me. He telephoned on 4 May, in the middle of the night (I had given him my home number), and asked if he could drop round there and then.

"Ten minutes later, he rang at the door. When I opened it, I thought at first glance that Serval was drunk, or drugged, but I soon grasped that it was fear which gave him that pale, wild-eyed look. He sank into a chair and gulped down a whole glass of gin.

"He had a thick brown envelope under his arm. He handed it to me:

"'I would like to ask you to keep this. I beg you, show it to no one! Put it in your safe. I know that it's the reason why my life is in danger. If anything ever happens to me, that's where you must scrabble around in order to understand.'

"I tried to calm him down, suggested that one of my men should act as his escort, but that seemed to make him even more afraid, and he made me promise that, whatever happened, I would not breathe a word of the whole business to anyone else. I asked him what he planned to do.

"'I don't know. I'll try to get back to Europe. But I am afraid that my enemies won't give me enough time.'

"I offered to bring forward my next trip to France by a few days (it had long been arranged for today), and to accompany him on the journey. The nearness of my departure seemed to agitate him a great deal. He stood up suddenly, and explained that he had to get back urgently. On the door-step he added, almost in a whisper:

"'Maybe it will all have been sorted out by 15 May. If not, too bad.'

"When he had gone, I put the envelope in my safe and went back to bed. Half an hour later, Serval telephoned again. His voice sounded strange, as if he were deciphering a text which he did not understand. He explained with emphases that were almost unbalanced that if, by the date of my departure (that is to say, by today), he had not asked me to return the envelope to him, then I should entrust it to you, and to you alone. He would get in touch with you directly to give all necessary instructions. I see that he didn't have time to do so between that last conversation and his disappearance, four days later."

"On the other hand," I pointed out, "he found time to play poker, as if there were nothing else on his mind."

"Perhaps that is part of the mystery which we must now unravel."

"What is there in the envelope?"

The Consul shrugged his shoulders.

"To all appearances, just the manuscript of his last book. I've only had time to leaf through it, and I got nothing much out of it. But you'll be much better able to read between the lines."

"What exactly do you want me to do? I'm no detective."

The Consul pushed a green ticket towards me across the table. It was a coat check, number 15597.

"When you leave, give this ticket to the cloakroom attendant. She will exchange it for a black leather briefcase. In the case, you will find the manuscript that Serval put in my hands, the first police reports and the Embassy file, and my own notes on the affair. But you really must not launch into an official investigation, as you are obviously not supposed to know anything. I shall be away for three weeks. That should leave you plenty of time to take the novel to pieces. That's all I am asking you to do: for I know you are fond of puzzles. If we take Serval at his word, then maybe the keys to this puzzle are hidden in the book. Your task is to find them."

CHAPTER TWO

Etampes

Lemarquis taught Latin and Greek and held teaching in low esteem. It was said that he introduced himself in those terms to his pupils every year for two decades, and he certainly did so when he came into his new III B class on the first Monday of October 1949. I remember him well: a short, thin man, with a tightly drawn face, a greenish skin, an untrustworthy look in his eye and a ghoulish smile, whose greatest pleasure in life seemed to be to make us conjugate twenty times over, in every person, tense and mood, "I do not copy out without understanding them sentences from Virgil given as examples in Gaffiot," "Thou dost not copy out without understanding them sentences from Virgil given as examples in Gaffiot," etc. But as for Stéphane Réal: zero.

I spent the whole afternoon and early evening trying in vain to find a memory of my supposed classmate, and in the process summoned up, with ever more obsessive precision, the details of the five endless school years that I had spent in that institution.

Collège Geoffroy-Saint-Hilaire drew its flock from seven tribes. The first, which made up the corps of day pupils, consisted of boys and girls whose parents were locals, or who lived locally: the baker's daughter (for the love of whom I later thought I would expire), the tobacconist's daughter, the five sons of Dr Chamier, the local tailor's son, the daughter of Monsieur Bombet, master draper and milliner, whose shop was called Capital Fashion, etc. The second, which made up almost all the day-boarders, were the bumpkins – horny-handed sons of the soil from the big farms of Beauce, from backwaters where the railway did not go: Sermaises, Verrières, Méréville, Angerville, Saclas, Maisse, Chalo-Saint-Mars, places which for me sounded quite exotic. The five other tribes, contributing in roughly equal measures to a good half of the school's complement, supplied the boarders who had all ended up, for one reason or another, at Etampes.

First there were the Parisians ("Paris swanks, thick as planks, Paris yob, shut yer gob"), slackers sacked from the "better" lycées in the capital or the inner suburbs (such as Lycée Lakanal at Sceaux, Lycée Hoche at Versailles), and whose despairing parents had resigned themselves to having their boys put down here just to get them through to the baccalaureate. Then came the Corsicans – not so much a group, more like a gang. They were all more or less cousins by blood or marriage, and it's probably only because one of them once happened to land at Etampes that all the others followed on, year after year. They were Paris Corsicans, of course, but quite distinct from Parisians. I remember one who said he had been a barman at the Hôtel Crillon and was kept by a mistress: he was called Dominique Salviati, and he always had a flick knife on him. There were two others, as well, called Pedrotti and Pedrocchi, whom the teachers forever muddled up.

Africa and Asia contributed the remainder. Every year, fifteen or twenty poor sods (whom we firmly believed were all "sons of chiefs") were dumped at Etampes from some French West African colony or other (Senegal or Cameroon, I believe). They were tall and strong, often of indeterminate age (one of them was reputed to be twenty-five), and terribly downcast. They suffered the harsh winters of Etampes and the school's puny heating system with stoic resignation, waiting desperately for time to pass, and only recovered a little of their *joie de vivre* at the approach of summer – and of the long holidays.

Fifteen or so other boarders came from North Africa, more particularly from Tunisia. It was to them that we felt closest, for they were even more skint than we could be – but whenever one of them got a postal order, he would shower us all straight away with cigarettes and chewing gum, or take us to The Royal, a fleapit in Rue des Vieux-Jésuites, which ran Westerns and gangster movies.

The last were the Indochinese. They kept to themselves and no one liked them. Only one acquired a degree of popularity, for his talent as a draughtsman. Using a pantograph, he made enlarged copies of pin-ups' faces from *Cinémonde* or from *Paris-Flirt* (a magazine which "bared it all" and which we hid under our mattresses in the dorm), and then took week upon week of evening study periods to polish the details and put in the shading. The final result was breathtakingly lifelike. He had amazing equipment, in particular a huge box of compasses and a kind of small chrome-plated sprayer with which he put a protective layer of varnish on his finished works of art. Most of the Indochinese (only towards the end of my years at Etampes did we start to call them Vietnamese) were scandalously rich, and lived in a style which we could barely imagine. They had splendid suits, made to measure by a tailor in Boulevard Saint-Michel. They went up to Paris every week, ate in restaurants, went to nightclubs, and, when they missed the last train on Sunday evenings, thought nothing of taking a taxi all the way back to Etampes.

I remembered that I still had a school photograph from Etampes in my things. I found it easily enough, at the bottom of a shoe box that I used for storage. The photograph was taken in 1951, when I was in fourth form. There are two teachers with the class – one must be Charbonel, the history-geography man, a fine figure of a superannuated athlete. He was famous for his laid-back manner, and he is still the only teacher I have ever seen (even since I crossed over to the other side, so to speak) who never had any kind of briefcase. All his lessons were written down on pieces of square-ruled, 14 × 17cm card, which he would extract nonchalantly from his breast pocket as he sat down at the desk. The cards were covered in extraordinarily tiny writing, and, in his notes for economic geography, the figures were entered in pencil, so he could erase and update them as new statistics became available. The other teacher is certainly Madame Borroni, the Italian mistress, who had only one student in our class, and who was supposed to have published a book on the satires of Ariosto (for which reason I got as far as my first baccalaureate without knowing the names of Dante, Petrarch or Tasso, but well aware that a certain Mr Ariosto had written satires; my German literature wasn't much hotter, even though German was supposed to be my second language: all that is left of it now is "Der-die-das,"

"Nouns-take-a-capital-letter," and
> Ich weiß nicht was soll es bedeuten
> Daß ich so traurig bin
> Ein Märchen aus alten Zeiten
> Das kommt mir nicht aus dem Sinn

rattled off as fast as possible without stopping for breath).

There are twenty-five pupils on the photograph of class IV B (one of the few pedagogic advantages of these schools in the outer Paris region was that classes were a little less overcrowded than in city schools). Apart from the teachers, everyone signed the photograph on the back, and some of the names which can still be deciphered bring back hazy memories: Bédollière, first name Emile, the clever lad – top of the class, with five first prizes in different subjects at the year's end. He was the son of a gendarme and he left the following year because his father had been transferred to Tarbes. I saw him again a couple of times later on, when he lived in Paris, in Boulevard Blanqui, in a student residence which had previously been a brothel (there were several student halls of that sort in those days). His bedroom was decorated like a ship's cabin, with trompe-l'oeil portholes giving a view of a south-sea island with coconut palms, sandy beaches, sailing boats in a creek, and straw huts. And I remember Ambroise Dupont and Auguste Dupouy, the inseparable bumpkins from Etréchy; and Aubry, a dentist's son, the dullest of the dullards from Paris, whose track crossed mine again twenty-five years later, at Veulles-les-Roses: he had become a television journalist. And Pierrette Lenoir, who sat the *agrégation* the same year as I did; and Saurin, called Crocodile by all and sundry, and Gratinaud, whose father belted him whenever he scored less than twelve out of twenty across the board and who, I learned years later, became a judge in a juveniles' court.

Some of the signatures are childish marks of identity made intentionally illegible with squiggles and curlicues. Others – Dubois, Dufour, Lanvallère – mean nothing to me now, nor do the corresponding faces bring any memories back. At all events, there's nothing that even faintly suggests Réal.

But other memories flood back, and it's impossible to stop the flow. The memory of my first arrival, in my parents' car, in early October: there was a fete at the fairground (it was Michaelmas, and, as I learned later, Saint Michael is the patron saint of Etampes); my first meal in the refectory, using the ration card which I had to hand to an old woman all draped in black, who was the headmaster's mother (I think the ration-card business lasted only a few weeks, it must have been the last vestige of post-war restrictions); my fear of the ragging inflicted on newcomers, my fear of the "seniors" which lasted almost the whole of my first year; Thursday afternoon outings to the Filoir sports ground, or to the woods behind Tour de Guinette, a ruined fortress which was supposed to have a real secret passage, or along a road with milestones shaped like shell-heads, commemorating the route taken by the victorious First Armoured Division of General Leclerc; the dismal returns on the Sunday evening train, with a pair of sheets and a week's clean underwear in my little cardboard suitcase, and the names of the railway stations between Brétigny and Etampes, shouted out in the dark and heard so many times that I can recite them with ease nearly thirty years after: Maroles-en-Hurepoix (during the Occupation, the Germans pronounced it *Maroless-enn-Hurapohix*), Chamarande, Bouray, Lardy, Etréchy; and the fey blond prefect we loathed and nicknamed Cuckold because he wore a yellow scarf; and the Corsican prefect who kept in his locker a piece of cheese several months old, which he had to tackle with a hammer; and the other prefect, Angelmarre, who was so poor that he made his shoe soles from wodges of art paper offcuts, and used bits of string dipped in black ink for laces . . .

Then it all came back, higgledy-piggledy: the banks of the Juine, Saint-Martin church with its tower than leans like Pisa's, the swimming pool at the end of the walk to Guinette, the little café in the station forecourt where the "seniors" pretended to be regulars; the tall, sinister building of "The Knacker's" which you saw from the train just before arriving at the town, set all on its own at the end of a long strip of waste land (the building is still there nowadays, unused but undemolished, next to a Simca factory and a button-bright housing development); cigs in the lav ("High Life," which we pronounced *Izhleef* as a joke, or perhaps out of ignorance, "Naja," "Elégantes," and another brand whose name I cannot recall but which came in a blue or sky-blue pack decorated with a gracious white horse-drawn coach); wanking contests in the little room next to the dorm where we had our lockers; valve-set radios, games of noughts and crosses, hangman, word-squares . . .

Names come back to me, names without faces: Turpin, Collière, Levasseur, Perechnikoff, Ben Zaoud, Big Chapuis and his little brother, Jay, the art master; and faces without names – teachers' faces, prefects' faces, boys' faces, fat pale faces, faces of hairy clowns proudly sporting their first moustache, faces of clodhoppers dressed up in their Sunday best, faces of shadows shivering from cold in the corridor where we queued up for the refectory; and memories of the places which made up our mental map: the big yard, the small yard, the covered gym, the shed, the physnatsci hall (and the very young science teacher who blushed all the time), the stairs to the dorm, the metalwork studio and woodwork studio, and the pair of bookends (a ghastly application of what was supposed to be "dove-tailing") which I took an entire year to bungle . . . I remember the sounds, the bell that rang at the end of each lesson, the noise we made with our clogs when we got into line in the corridor, the shouting in the yard during play, the hullabaloo in the refectory, and even the sound of the silence we made when the deputy head came in. I remember the taste of lentils and pease pudding, the smell of urine and of cauliflower . . .

Shreds and tatters of the past come back to mind at a stroke. In one of those years (was it fourth form?) I spent three whole weeks drawing a huge map of Ancient Rome; another time, we all tried to solve an impossible problem. You trace six squares onto a sheet of paper to represent three dwellings and three utilities, for gas, water and electricity respectively: the problem is to supply each of the dwellings with all the utilities without any supply line crossing any other. That made nine lines. We tried every which way. It wasn't really very hard to get to eight, but with depressing and inexorable consistency the ninth line bumped every time into one of the others. Or else, for several weeks, there was a craze for sending each other coded letters, using "grids" which had to be applied four times over in different ways (as Jules Verne explains at the start of *Mathias Sandorf*) to reveal the solution.

Several times in the course of writing down these memories which have surged up in tangled bunches I have caught myself, with pen poised, drifting off for minutes at a time, into a persistent daydream in which I could almost see myself, if I just closed my eyes, standing once again in those playgrounds, queuing in those squalid corridors, sitting in those classrooms with their iron-barred windows. I was back playing prisoner's base, sitting through prize day in the refectory decorated for the occasion with three faded paper ribbons, suffering in the "group display" at the Seine-et-Oise Junior Gym Gala. I could see the art room again, with its plaster busts and the high pedestal on which the teacher carefully laid out an alarm clock, a flask and two apples (introduction to still life), and the geography room where Agricultural France, Physical Europe and Black Africa hung on the wall, and the dorm with the peculiar hutch where the duty prefect slept, and the study room with our padlocked personal lockers right at the back; and it was as if I really had been taken back into those dull and sweaty hours, into that semi-prisoner's life measured out from week to week, from dictation to dictation, from test to test, from games period to music lesson, from delta equals be squared minus four hay see to

O Lord of heaven and earth and sea

To Thee all praise and glory be

I had to pinch myself hard to come back down to earth, to Grianta in the sultry month of May, to the curfew, to the President-for-Life and his chummy, chubby face, to lunch with the Consul, and to the mystery of Robert Serval's disappearance.

Funnily enough, I can't really see Serval as an old boy from Etampes, despite not having any idea what old Etampians look like. I imagine him more as one of those types from Saint-Louis-de-Gonzague or the Ecole Alsacienne who sit the *Concours général*, get their philosophy essay published in *Le Figaro*, become stars of the sixth and end up top at Ecole normale supérieure; or else as the opposite, as a lad from the country who'd given and gotten plenty of punches in village scrums before teaching himself to read all by himself from an ancient almanac with wood-cut

vignettes; at any rate, as someone from an exceptional background, so as to match the somewhat overheroic and obviously
naive idea which I have of a writer of thrillers living as a recluse
in a tropical grand hotel.

CHAPTER THREE

The Crypt

"Serval soon found the Marktendörin. He had himself shown
to the office of the deputy director, to whom he handed Dr Ge-
strigleben's letter. Guards escorted him through a labyrinth of
sparkling clean, steely cold corridors, and had him wait in a small
room divided in two by a huge panel of bulletproof glass. A few
minutes later, a door opened into the other half of the room, and
Vichard came in. On seeing him, Serval could not stop himself
starting with surprise. His old school friend was wearing a col-
larless grey pea jacket and poor felt slipper-socks, and, with his
head almost entirely shaved, he looked like an ailing old man."

That is the beginning of Serval's novel. Its title is *The Crypt*.
It takes the form of a manuscript of 130 neatly typed pages, free
of corrections, deletions and additions of any kind. There is a
quite peculiar black and white photograph gummed on the front
cover, which is just a sheet of shiny black plastic without the name
of the book, or of the author. I presume that what it represents
is a painted signboard, bearing a rather primitive but charming
sign, that must be posted somewhere in the southern depths of
Morocco. It depicts a semi-arid landscape, with a few traces of
vegetation and a clump of trees in the far distance, against a background of sand dunes and hills. In the left foreground is a smiling
native face, cut off at the bust by the picture frame; the native
holds the reins of a camel entering from the left, with only the
neck and head of the beast visible in profile. In the middle ground,
four camel-drivers ride their mounts towards the right. Against
the sky, a long arrow points rightwards beneath the legend sten-
cilled in large letters:

TIMBUKTOO 52 DAYS

and above that, a legend in Arabic which presumably says the same thing, the other way round.

The Crypt is a detective novel, a detective novel in two parts, the second of which meticulously undoes everything that the first part tries to establish – a classical device of many enigma-novels, taken here to an almost absurd extreme.

The detective is called Robert Serval and speaks of himself in the third person. This morning I went to the library of the Alliance Française, which has in stock eleven of Serval's twenty-one published works (I took the opportunity to borrow three of them, *The Giletti Affair, The Corpse Had One Eye Open,* and *The Colonel's Secret*), which enabled me to establish that it was his standard practice. As with Ellery Queen and others, the author's pseudonym is the same as the name of his hero, save that Ellery Queen masks two writers (Fred Dannay and Manfred B Lee), whereas Stéphane Réal alias Robert Serval is but one man.

The action of *The Crypt* is set almost entirely in the city of Gotterdam, the capital of a Nordic, not to say polar country called Fernland. It is winter and very cold. Serval alludes to snowdrifts three metres deep, a frozen river, blizzards hitting the city and bringing it to a complete standstill within minutes. These heightened descriptions of a harsh climate are almost obscene, and even momentarily incomprehensible, when read in the sweltering torpor of Grianta, where it's impossible to see snow or to call it to mind. From the instant when I set foot on the blistering tarmac of Saint Lucia airport, just over eighteen months ago, the mere existence of my sheepskin jacket, and of everything else with the remotest resemblance to a scarf or bodywarmer, receded into the realms of the unthinkable. I suppose Serval chose to write about a virtually subpolar city to conjure the demons of this place, as if, in order to acquire distance from the unrelenting furnace of Grianta, he had had to delve for safety into memories of Canadian "dusters" and Norwegian blizzards (which paradoxically produces the same kind of life indoors, in bittercold air conditioning here, in overheated houses there). At any rate, Serval seems to have had his own sly fun laying on the woollens and furs: all his characters wear astrakhan shapskas over thick woolly mufflers, silk under-gloves beneath massive mittens, long underpants, fur-lined boots and sealskin capes, in spite of which icicles form in nostrils and on moustaches as soon as their owners put their noses outside; more seriously, road sweepers collect up a few already rock-hard corpses every morning.

The affair narrated in the book had begun a few months before the opening.

The naval attaché at the French Embassy, Lieutenant Com-mander Rémi Rouard, has died in circumstances which give rise to suspicions of foul play. On his way home late at night from a reception at the residence of a business magnate, Einar Svendsen, Rouard apparently lost control of his car, missed a bend, hit a barrier, and tumbled about sixty metres to the bottom of a ravine known as Devil's Rift. The car exploded. Fragments of twisted metal and pieces of burnt and torn flesh and bone were found in a radius of thirty metres.

The supposition of a road accident (which no reader would seriously entertain) is only made in order to be shot down fort-with. The corniche along Devil's Rift is perilously narrow, but at the relevant hour of the night it was "absolutely deserted," and Rouard was justifiably reputed to have *earned his pips* as a driver. Obviously he could have been drinking over the limit in the course of the soirée, but the reader is told straight out that Rouard had spent the whole evening in a state of exemplary sobri-ety. Moreover, in conversation with several guests, he appears to have alluded to threats which, he said, had been made just recently.

Preliminary analyses of the wreckage of the car quickly con-vince the investigators that they are dealing with a case of sab-otage. Closer inspection proves irrefutably, first, that the brakes and steering had been tampered with, and, second, that an explo-sive device had been placed in the vehicle. So it must have been manslaughter with premeditated intent: first-degree murder.

The enquiry is led by Detective Inspector Frederick Blackstone. As the victim was a French national in government service abroad, the Foreign Office also sends out one of our men, Inspector Derville.

Rouard arrived at Svendsen's at nine forty-five p.m. and was one of the last to leave, at four a.m. His car must have been interfered with during that period. According to experts, even allowing for the time it might have taken to find Rouard's car in the underground car park of the Svendsen residence, anyone with barely more than basic mechanical knowledge and the necessary tools (to wit, a set of box spanners of the sort you will find in any standard car-repair kit) would have needed no more than fifteen minutes at the most to alter the adjustment of the steering column and to empty the braking system of a sufficient proportion of fluid. I shall skip various secondary details, including the reconstitution of the evening's events and the checking of everyone's movements. In any case, it becomes obvious, around page 30, that of the thirty-three people attending the reception, twenty guests and thirteen hosts (the six members of the Svendsen family, with their seven permanent or temporary staff), only four could have committed the crime. As it is a detective story, the reader is hardly surprised to learn that all four can also be shown to have more or less good reasons to wish Rouard dead. Then four short chapters introduce us to the four suspects.

"Cherchez la femme"

The "woman" is Anne Svendsen, the third of the mogul's four daughters. She had been out of the room for about half an hour. Her current paramour, a young Argentinian architect by the name of Di Magalco, had looked for but not found her in the drawing rooms and kitchens. She claims she had gone up to her room to use the telephone, but no one can corroborate her claim. More pointedly, the girl at the cloakroom in the hall, who could not have missed seeing Anne go up the stairs to the bedrooms, asserts that she saw nothing of the kind. We also learn that Anne Svendsen had been Rouard's lover for over a year and that they had broken up only a few weeks before the party.

"The Ugly American"
About a year beforehand, Fernland announced that it was minded to order a set of sophisticated torpedo boats for its coastguard fleet. A little later, the Minister of Interior, speaking at the inauguration of the Higher Police Academy, implied that the French contender, the modified Arethusa 234F code-name "Martine," carrying four MCB 1000S launchers and RAPR ballistic warheads, stood a good chance of winning the order. Shortly thereafter, Lt.-Cdr. Rouard led the French team that conducted the ensuing and very tortuous negotiations. Questions on the vessels themselves were quickly resolved, but a lot more time was taken over equipment specifications, especially the availability of spares and maintenance contracts. However, it was all on the brink of being signed and sealed when, six weeks before the mystery occurred, Gotterdam abruptly requested deferring the option expiry date by three months. It was not easy for the French side to take this decision as anything other than a diplomatic rebuff, and it seems to have been made just a few days after the arrival at the American Embassy in Gotterdam of a new Trade Counsellor by the name of Jo Barrett.

Barrett had been at the Svendsen reception, but was unable to give an account of his movements. He said he had sauntered from one room to another, had had a drink at the pool, had chatted in the music room. According to several servants and guests, Rouard had been looking for Barrett at several different times, but the American had not been where people thought he would be.

"The Chinaman"
The Chinaman is none other than Einar Svendsen himself. The nickname comes from his extensive business connections in the Far East. He is presented as an energetic and brutal man, pasha and despot combined.

Einar Svendsen had spent most of the evening playing whist with his usual partners, Jakobson the banker, Van Proet, the editor of *Ö Färtkrift* ("Progress"), and Stanley Dahlström, an under-secretary at the Department of Transport. During a break in play, Svendsen had gone to his car to fetch a copy of Hazlitt's *Characters of Shakespeare's Plays* which he had just acquired from a dealer at Hudiksvall and which he wanted to show to Jakobson, a fellow bibliophile. In fact, he was gone for over twenty minutes; his partners had begun to get impatient and had already sent a servant to look for him when he returned. The book-dealer was questioned and confirmed that he had indeed sold Svendsen the Hazlitt, but had done so more than a month before. Why was the book still in the glovebox of Svendsen's car? Why had Svendsen, despite his sciatica, gone to get it himself, instead of sending a servant? And why had he taken nearly twenty-five minutes to do so, when five would have been ample? These three questions, which the businessman persisted in answering evasively and dishonestly (claiming, to begin with, that he had come back inside ten minutes, then saying that there was no light in the car park, or that he had got stuck between two doors by a prowler whom no one could find) would perhaps not have sufficed to make Svendsen a prime suspect; but Blackstone soon learns from a servant that, in a violent quarrel with his daughter Anne a few moments before the first guests arrived, Svendsen had let fly against that damned *Frössfrätzer* ("frog eater") who was forever putting a spanner in his works.

"Quite an affair for a chargé d'affaires"

César Vichard de Moutiers is the First Secretary at the French Embassy. The accredited Ambassador, Devaux, spends more than two thirds of his time away from his post. A qualified economist and geographer, Devaux is considered an authority on all aspects of working marl- and silica-rich soils. His specialist knowledge makes him a much sought after expert at national and international farming conferences, so Vichard stands in for him at Gotterdam most of the time.

That evening, Vichard had opened an exhibition of Masterpieces of French Orology, then attended act one of *Öd Döpfelunbästijk* (Marivaux's *La Double Inconstance*) performed by the Royal Theatre of Gotterdam, before getting to Svendsen's at ten p.m. He left half an hour later, saying he would call back. He did return to the party, in fact, towards a quarter to one. Maybe he expected the party to be at its peak at that time, but in truth it was already winding down; at all events, the few people he talked to found him rather downcast, even gloomy. When Blackstone questioned him on his movements between ten thirty p.m. and twelve forty-five a.m., he declared that in his official capacity he had attended a dinner being given by the Cultural Attaché for a French writer on a lecture tour of Fernland. But all present at that dinner are sure that Vichard stayed there no more than fifteen minutes.

Vichard is, or rather, was very close to Rouard. They had often had the same postings, at Smolensk, Brunswick and Vienna. They share a huge villa at Flåksund, a fishing village twenty kilometres outside Gotterdam. Some have drawn the hasty conclusion that they also shared Anne Svendsen.

In the ensuing chapters, Blackstone explores these four leads with varying degrees of success and flair. Is it a crime of passion? A revenge killing? Or a murky case of industrial espionage? Nothing emerges very clearly until Blackstone makes some "interesting discoveries."

First, he learns that Anne Svendsen is a *belle-de-jour* in a brothel known to its regulars by the name of The Crypt. It seems she has met Barrett there several times. But the most astounding thing is that the brothel belongs covertly to Svendsen, who uses his daughter in it to obtain information on various industrial and commercial operations.

At this stage of the investigation, Blackstone begins to wonder if Einar Svendsen and Barrett haven't simply conspired to get rid of Rouard and his French boats, and to carve up the deal (conservatively reckoned to be worth not far short of one hundred million pounds) between them.

But a new clue soon shifts suspicion onto Vichard.

One of Blackstone's assistants carries out a routine enquiry to check the statements of the First Secretary. He peruses the log of Vichard's official car, and sees that on the evening of the crime the vehicle had covered almost fifty kilometres more than what Vichard's account of his movements would add up to. When questioned, the driver reveals that, on arriving at the residence of the

Cultural Attaché, Vichard had sent him off to bed, and kept the car himself.

Blackstone noses around the villa of Vichard and Rouard, and learns from a neighbour that Vichard had returned home just before midnight on the evening of the Svendsen party. He hadn't even switched off the ignition, he had just gone into the garage and come out again straightaway with a wooden box which he put in the boot of his car.

At his second interview, Vichard confesses that he had gone back to Flåksund to fetch a crate of champagne, and he could even say what brand it was: Périer-Lagrange.

The crate of champagne gets Vichard into endless, inextricable trouble. Perhaps the diplomat really had taken it to Svendsen's, but it doesn't seem that it was drunk there, and at all events it left no trace in the memories of all who had been at the party. Then Vichard explains, but only to tie himself into awful knots, that the champagne was the consequence of a wager which Ynge, the youngest of the Svendsen daughters, had won. She had reminded him of it quite forcefully earlier on in the evening, and so he had promised to call back at his house to collect the crate before returning to the party. He had then looked for Rouard amongst the throng, to help him bring up the crate. Rouard was deep in conversation with another guest on the terrace, and made it obvious that Vichard was disturbing him. The First Secretary came back a while later, but Rouard was no longer there. In the end, he decided to put the crate onto the goods lift all by himself, but this time, the crate disappeared! It was getting late, Vichard was sleepy, and the party was pretty dull; so he decided to go home. Three hours later, Rouard met his death . . .

There is nothing that proves clearly that the crate of champagne contained the explosive device placed in Rouard's car. In the meantime, however, the specialists have retrieved a sufficient number of fragments of the bomb to identify its type with certainty. Although it was only a modest device, it would have been too large to be carried around without attracting attention. But it would have fitted neatly into a twelve-bottle crate, as used for champagne, for instance.

The device used was a French-made percussion mine of an already rather obsolete kind called CDP 411.38. Developed during the war in Indochina, it was specifically designed for use in the shallow and narrow waterways used by Vietminh junks, in places where magnetic charges would not have been at all effective. It has been little used since then, except on a few occasions in Algeria and Chad, but stocks still exist in some French naval ordnance stores.

It so happened, in fact, that several of these mines had been touring the Nordic countries recently in an itinerant exhibition, entitled *The Glories of Naval Warfare*, celebrating the fortieth anniversary of the Battle of Narvik. One of the exhibits (minus detonator, in fact, but the specialists seem to treat that as a minor detail) had been "lost" somewhere between Gotterdam and Löden. There is a lot of correspondence about the disappearance of CDP 411.38. The final report from the Inspector of Military Police concludes that it was "theft perpetrated by a fanatical collector," but, given the circumstances of Rouard's death, it is obvious that the case will have to be reopened. The names of Devaux, Vichard and Rouard appear in the file many times already.

At this point in the investigation, it seems to have been established, at least in the minds of the police, that this is a case concerning French nationals and no others; so Blackstone is replaced as head of the team by Derville, and the French Foreign Office soon sends out two special investigators, Boutin and Vergnaud, to back him up.

Things now take a very bad turn for Vichard: Rouard's sister bursts onto the Gotterdam scene and gives Derville two letters which her brother had sent her some time before his death, but which she had only opened a month later, a month too late, on her return from holiday.

In the first of the letters, Rouard paints a singularly gloomy picture of his position at Gotterdam, and tells his sister of the suspicions that have begun to haunt him. He writes, amongst other things:

"Of all the postings I have had, Gotterdam, despite its climate, is probably the one where I could have settled down with greatest ease and success. But my relations with CV have got steadily worse over the last months. He persists in making me feel as though I would be nothing if I did not have his protection; his pathological jealousy and despotism are becoming more and more intolerable. He meddles in my professional and private life, spies on my every movement, demands an account of everything I do. The day before yesterday, he forbade me to carry on with the sale of the Arethusa. He says he is taking over the negotiations himself But I have reasons – even if I can't prove them yet – to believe that his involvement will have a catastrophic effect. I don't yet know how I am going to handle things, whether I should alert the Military Police straightaway, or wait. He's got himself into a position where he can manipulate everybody here. No one would believe me. There's only Devaux whom I could really trust, but he won't be back until October, and I fear it will be too late then. Etc."

The second letter was a brief note mailed on the day before the accident:

"I'll be in Paris on Sunday. Book me a room in your name at the Hôtel de Nantes. Call Boulot and ask him to collect me at Roissy, from flight SAS 223, at seven p.m."

Boulot is the name of one of the Military Police detectives who had worked on the case of the disappearing CDP 411.38.

Confronted with the evidence piling up against him, Vichard retreats into an absurd defensive position. He just goes on denying everything en bloc, repeating that he does not understand anything of what he is being told: he has never crossed swords with Rouard, à propos of Anne Svendsen or of anything else at all, he has never purloined an explosive device nor any other kind of weapon, he has never doubted Rouard's abilities, never even thought of conducting the torpedo boat negotiations in his stead, never sought to undermine those negotiations, etc.

But the presumptive evidence is so great that in the end Vichard is officially charged, and remanded in custody at Marktendörin prison. The Foreign Office gives him permission to bring out an old friend to Gotterdam to conduct further enquiries. The First Secretary's childhood friend is called Robert Serval.

The whole first part of this novel is thus in fact a flashback during which Vichard, Blackstone, Derville and the other characters have been reconstituting the main episodes of the drama and of the subsequent investigation for Serval's benefit.

In the final chapter, Vichard declares his innocence once again, and begs Serval to unmask the evil plot which has made him its victim.

CHAPTER FOUR

Counter-enquiry

Vichard's protestations of innocence against all the apparent evidence whets Serval's interest and stimulates his flair more than anything else. However, although he has an intuition of the truth almost from the start, he will need all the ingenuity of a master sleuth to come up with the proof. Every time some piece of the puzzle begins to come into focus, it fades away in a blur, evaporates in a wisp of thin and dubious haze, or gets bogged down in paperwork without sense or substance. Interrogation follows interrogation, statement follows statement – and each one brings more tiny contradictions to light which further obfuscate the ungraspable, unseeable reality which the investigators are trying so hard to reconstitute. For instance, one guest at the party suddenly recalls that a maître d'hôtel with a puce complexion served him "first-rate champagne"; but when he is asked about it, Svendsen replies grumpily that he had forbidden once and for all time for anyone to bring that repulsive beverage into his house, that he holds it to be a poison, that his maître d'hôtel is a teetotaller with a markedly pale complexion, and that the boozy b . . . was obviously confusing his party with the following day's reception at the British Embassy. Then another guest thinks he is sure he had seen Barrett and Rouard go out together at about eleven thirty p.m. Day by day, reports, specialist evidence, statements and interview transcripts pile up on Derville's desk, making it harder and harder to see anything clearly.

However, in a sense which could be called abstract, theoretical or logical, the key to the enigma is simple. If Vichard is telling the truth, then one thing is clear: that Rouard had lied in the letters he wrote. Now Serval *knows* that Vichard has told him the truth.

Therefore Rouard had been lying. Why had he lied? What was it that made him think he could prove that Vichard was a traitor? Did Barrett plant the idea in his mind? Or Anne? Or else what? It would be nice to imagine that one of the other three suspects killed Rouard in such a way as to get Vichard accused of the murder, but how could he (or she) have obtained Rouard's complicity in deceiving others about his own death? Otherwise it would have to be assumed either that Rouard had managed to pass off suicide as a murder committed by Vichard (but how? and why?) – or that Rouard was not dead!

Serval moves into Vichard's villa. He searches it from top to bottom. He also goes through Rouard's part of the house. He toothcombs the medicine chests, the wardrobes, the cellars. He does not know what he is looking for. From his bedroom window, he looks out at the little fishing port all covered in snow. All he can see of the low-roofed houses are a few slates and smoking chimneys. A knot of men wrapped in grey furs haul a long, silvery boat onto the shore. For maybe the hundredth time, Serval writes on a scrap of paper:

WHO

HOW

WHY

WITH WHOM

MASQUERADING AS

DIVERTING SUSPICION ONTO

Then he crosses it out again angrily, crumples the scrap into a ball, and throws it into the waste-paper bin.

Snow has been falling for three days and three nights. In the town, traffic has stopped. Shops have shut, schools and offices have closed down. Appeals are broadcast on radio for people to stay indoors. Night falls at three p.m. During the day, there are power cuts. Telephones are often out of order.

Everything is in suspension. The enquiry has run out of steam.

Oddly enough (but in fact it is not odd at all), at this point a book crops up which will permit Serval to solve the puzzle.

It is another detective story. It is called *The Magistrate is the*

Murderer, and its author's name is Lawrence Wargrave. The book had fallen behind the radiator in Rouard's bathroom. It is one of those slim popular novels in what were generally weekly series, of the sort brought out in their hundreds and thousands in the 1930s. It belonged to a series called *Murder About*, published by Smith and Co. On the colour-printed jacket is a conventional key-hole cutout, through which a hotel bedroom can be seen – a bed with a red cretonne spread, a washbasin purporting to be hidden behind a flowery pink screen, an armchair upholstered in green fabric – where an entirely bald, broken-nosed man of about fifty, dressed in a heavy, black, fur-collared overcoat, is strangling a young woman wearing a black and pink lace negligé.

That is the first episode in the book. M Tissier, an examining magistrate from Paris, visits Tonnerre (Yonne) on business, and puts up at the Hôtel de Sens. In the middle of the night he is awakened by screaming from the bedroom next door. M Tissier witnesses the drama portrayed on the jacket through the keyhole of the communicating door between his bedroom and the one next to it. But when he finally manages to rouse the night porter, the murderer has long since vanished into thin air.

The victim is soon identified as a callgirl by the name of Angèle, more precisely a taxi-girl who normally worked from a club in the Saint-Séverin quarter of Paris. Her pimp is a former American marine, and a wrestler to boot, called Fly, and his description matches the one given by Tissier exactly. But when Fly is arrested a fortnight later in Paris, he gives a cast-iron alibi, and the case against him is dropped.

Over the following weeks, the police begin to get letters from Tissier, who tells them of threats made against him by Fly. An inspector is detailed to shadow the magistrate and to keep an eye on his safety, but that doesn't stop him from being kidnapped, at eleven a.m., from in front of the Hôtel de Bourgogne, at the junction of Rue de Grenelle and Rue de Bourgogne.

In deep of night, the police burst into Fly's villa at Le Pecq. Fly is there, and seems to have been awakened from deep sleep. The officers show their search warrant, and proceed to go through the house with a toothcomb. They find a thick envelope containing photographs of Tissier in a night-table drawer. There are plenty of fingerprints on the envelope and the photographs – Fly's, and other people's, including those of a nightclub photographer who will later step into the witness box to tell how Fly had hired him to tail Tissier and to take shots of him in various places at various times of day.

The cement floor of the cellar has recently been scrubbed clean, but the bloodstains remain perceptible all the same. The police also retrieve a chainsaw from the coalheap; its teeth are clogged with matter which is soon shown to be human. The clinker in the boiler is still hot; lab tests show that a body had been incinerated. Lastly, three whitish splinters stuck in the grate are identified at the trial by Tissier's dentist as coming from the magistrate's ceramic crowns.

Fly looks on in blank and terrified amazement as these discoveries unfold before him. When he manages to get a grip on himself, he tries to explain that he had spent the whole day with a walking-stick enthusiast, who had taken him to Pithiviers to see his extraordinary collection, then to lunch at Fontainebleau, then to see another collector with equally fabulous specimens at Coulommiers, after which all three of them went to Ermenonville to have a slap-up dinner. The follow-on is even more muddled. Apparently Fly didn't realise he would be taken home, and took a while to grasp that his car had stayed at Pithiviers since the morning. But the white Mercedes is in the garage of his villa at Le Pecq; the bullet hole from the shot fired by Tissier's police guard is perfectly visible in the bodywork; and the walking-stick fanatics from Pithiviers and Coulommiers inexorably resist being found. In short, the pimp is arrested, charged, remanded in custody, tried, convicted and executed for the murder of examining magistrate Tissier, without ever managing to persuade anyone at all that he is innocent. Even his lawyer is convinced that Fly was lying all along the line.

In the final chapter, M Tissier, slightly altered in appearance, explains to the author, Lawrence Wargrave (who writes as "I" in the novel and introduces himself as "a student of criminology following the case for his practical"), how, "with the help of a few accomplices" (an invocation of little substance, made to permit all subsequent objections to be set aside), he had stage-managed his own demise by first seeking out the soft spot, the "fad" which would enable him to trap Fly most effectively, and would leave him almost a whole day's free run of the pimp's car and house. Stuffed to the gills with rich food and first-rate wine (and maybe a sleeping tablet or two), Fly was only brought back home in time to meet his accusers. All the rest was just misleading leads and false false teeth.

Instinct tells Serval on the spot that Rouard had used *The Magistrate is the Murderer*. He hadn't necessarily taken his "idea" from it (the idea itself, that of inventing a real culprit for the wrong crime, is really rather ordinary and schematic, and no more stimulating or difficult than finding the wrong culprit for a real crime), but there was a common method or organising principle – not something just bolted on to the puzzle, but a principle, adapted to a particular situation.

If the nub of the deception lies in letters written by the victim to point the finger at a culprit, as it does in *The Magistrate is the Murderer* (what could appear more authentic than letters written by a person deceased? can the dead lie?), Rouard, none the less, must have tackled the problem of his own physical disappearance and reappearance by means quite different from those of his literary model; for if what had been found at the bottom of Devil's Rift was not Rouard, whence came the little bits of corpse that had been collected? And where was the real Rémi Rouard now?

Serval goes back to the enquiry with this really quite flimsy scenario in mind. In what are probably the best pages of the book, the sleuth tries to imagine what he would have done had he been in the Naval Attaché's shoes, and slips step by step into the skin of an imaginary self-annihilator.

It is perfectly obvious that a sixty-metre fall to the bottom of a ravine is quite enough to ensure the death of the individual concerned. A bomb in addition could only have been intended to make identification of the corpse impossible or at worst very dubious.

Serval-detective announces this plain and obvious point in such a matter-of-fact way that the reader wonders why Serval-author had not allowed any of the other characters in the book to have the same inkling before him. It raises two questions:

First, since he could not make himself disappear entirely (by fire, acid, drowning, etc.), how could Rouard have estimated reliably that the combined effects of the "natural" explosion of the car as it hit the bottom and the arranged explosion of the CDP 411.38 would be to leave only a few fragments of the "victim's" flesh and bone, providing sufficient material (such as teeth) for identification but no unpredictable remnants which would allow it to be identified as a dummy corpse?

Second, how, precisely, had the identification of the remains been made? There had been no regular autopsy. What lab tests had been undertaken? With what results?

The second question has a relatively straightforward answer. As a matter of routine in the enquiry conducted jointly by the Gotterdam police and the French Embassy, samples of organic matter found at the scene of the incident ("fragments, shards and traces of bone, skin, cardiac tissue, nails, blood, viscera, lymph glands and vitreous humour") and a broken piece of a dental bridge were dispatched to Paris by private bag.

Since the Marhenbey scandal (after the name of the French Ambassador to the Holy See who had faked his own abduction in collusion with the Triestine Police), the medical records of all civil servants on overseas postings are kept centrally in Paris. The returns from the Forensic Medical Centre were comparatively definite: "There is a high degree of probability that the specimens subjected to tests came from the body of the former Naval Attaché." The "high degree of probability" naturally counted as certainty in Gotterdam, where everyone took it for granted that Rouard really had died in his car. But when he gives this part of the file closer scrutiny, Serval makes a strange discovery. The counter-foil of Gotterdam's analysis request and the Forensic Medical Centre's reply slip do not match completely. For instance, the FMC's slip lists specimens of liver tissue and muscle which do not figure in the Gotterdam dispatch; yet it does not mention the traces of lymph gland and vitreous humour which seem to have been sent (and the reactions of these to the Lauzanne-Tavistock test would have been particularly informative). Serval's cross-checking shows that the FMC tested *different* samples from those which Gotterdam sent, and which never arrived!

I'll summarise briefly the moves which this discovery sets in train. On the evening of the 2nd (two days after the death, if you can still call it that), the Deputy Director of the FMC, Thermin, and the head of the Northern Europe desk at the Foreign Office, Souchevort, were alerted by telephone (Vichard's call) that a special bag would arrive on the 3rd, at six p.m., by the hand of the chief steward of flight AF 161, Gotterdam–Paris via Oslo and Copenhagen. Next morning, Thermin's secretary had a call from Souchevort, who asked her to let Thermin know that he would fetch the bag himself from the airport police; she also got the same message from Thermin. By these means, a "Foreign Office Official" possessing all the requisite permits and passes was able to present himself to the Roissy airport police shortly after flight AF 161 landed and to take possession of the special bag in absolute and entire accordance with the law.

All diplomats above junior rank serving abroad are acquainted with the procedures, and it is perfectly conceivable that Rouard could have planned, set up and got away with a substitution of that kind.

In order to answer the first of his questions, however, Serval finds himself pursuing somewhat tight-lipped informants in circles vaguely related to the espionage and counter-intelligence services. In the end he finds out that before being posted to Smolensk Vichard and Rouard both underwent what was stated, or rather understated, to be "special training." One course module, taught at the FMC (where it was nicknamed "strawberry jam"), dealt with the use and reliability of biological, anatomical and path. lab. tests in identifying the victims of plane crashes and bomb blasts.

Furthermore, an article existed from way back, written by two engineers from the Bizerta ordnance base, Chappuis & Gelé, and entitled "Destructive Effects of the CDP 411.38," in *Army and Navy Equipment Review* (1952). The Embassy had a full run of the journal.

Serval now turned his attention to how Rouard might have got himself out of Fernland after having launched his well-prepared vehicle into the abyss of Devil's Rift.

Less than five hundred metres from the scene of the incident stands the smartest hotel in Gotterdam, The Crest, a nineteen-story building towering over the fjord which shelters the city.

Serval goes through the hotel's guest list and fairly soon lights upon the name of Julien Labbé.

The "crash" had happened on the night of Friday to Saturday, 29–30 September. Julien Labbé had checked in at the The Crest in the evening of 28 September, arriving from the airport by taxi after a flight, so he claimed, from Hamburg. On 29 September, he had used his room telephone to book a Citroën CX or equivalent from Hertz, and asked for the car to be left for him in the hotel car park. He had said he intended to drive to Copenhagen over-night, and to drop the car off there. Since M. Julien Labbé was a Hartz Club member, the rental was agreed without any fuss; the hirer brought the car (a Volvo) to The Crest at around nine p.m. and left the keys and papers with hotel reception. Around five a.m. M. Labbé, who had settled his bill the previous night with a credit card, took the car keys from his pigeon hole and departed.

No Julien Labbé figures on the passenger manifest of the Ham-burg–Gotterdam flight on 28 September. The passport number given (233184259) is false, and the address (7, Rue de Quatrefages) does not exist. The credit cards were not forgeries, however, and were supported by current account number 70336P at the Comptoir Commercial du Crédit, which had a positive balance of 271,328.53.French francs. The balance had been withdrawn and the account closed on 4 October.

In the last chapter of *The Crypt*, Serval summons Blackstone, Derville and their sidekicks to the French Embassy. He sums up:

"'Everything leads me to the conclusion that Rouard and Labbé are one and the same person. I must say that, from a strictly tech-nical point of view, the whole operation was carried out with masterly skill. The motive of the crime is probably related to the negotiations for which Rouard was responsible. But it will not be easy to demonstrate that he took a cut, from Barrett or from

Svendsen, for having sabotaged the French deal. As for discovering where he has gone to ground with his fistful of dollars . . .'

"'At any rate,' Derville put in, 'we can't maintain the charge against Vichard. The facts which Serval has brought to light exonerate him entirely.'

"The others nodded their agreement. Serval alone seemed not to share the certainty.

"'Unless . . .'

"All eyes turned towards the detective."

CHAPTER FIVE

Hypotheses

The entire adventure ends with a bleeping query, for the eyes that turn look towards a void: the following page of the book is blank, and it is the last. But you don't have to be a genius to guess what Serval (the detective-hero) had in mind and to finish his sentence for him:

"'. . . unless Vichard stage-managed the murder so that he would seem to be the prime suspect in the early stages of investigation, but, by proclaiming his innocence to his lifelong friend, would manage to set in train a second enquiry, in the course of which re-examination of the clues which had seemed stacked against him and the unearthing of new ones (the novel so conveniently dissimulated behind the bathroom radiator, the false FMC files, the Crest Hôtel, Julien Labbé, etc.) would make the contrary seem true, namely that it was he, Vichard, who was the victim of a machination plotted by Rouard . . .'"

It is not unusual for Serval to construct his novels in this manner. He pulls off the same kind of coup in two of the other three which I have read: just when the solution is found, another, completely different solution is thrown away in a few lines, so that the last twist of the tale, its final reversal, concluding surprise, ultimate revelation and punchline leaves the puzzled or fascinated reader with two equally plausible and entirely irreconcilable hypotheses.

I am not sure what to think of this detective story. Personally, I rather lean towards old Crozet's view—ingenious, but underdone. It sounds as if the writer had thought up an absolutely brilliant plot (something like Alphonse Allais's *It wasn't him! It wasn't her!*), but then cooked it to his regular recipe, paying insufficient attention to the details, perhaps kidding himself that he could gull the reader with "Lauzanne-Tavistock tests" and "destructive effects of the CDP" into swallowing whole the story of a murder without a corpse. To be sure, he is bright enough to hint at the very end that maybe it was really Vichard who had pulled all the strings, but that solution is barely touched on, and it would be very difficult to give it any substance. (To mention just one problem that would arise: if Rouard really was at the bottom of Devil's Rift, then who was the Labbé who drove off the Volvo? So Vichard had accomplices? Pretty weak, really.)

Anyway, I'm not supposed to be writing a reader's report on *The Crypt*, I'm supposed to be deciphering the clues it is supposed to contain to the apparently real disappearance from Grianta of Robert Serval, alias Stéphane Réal.

"If anything ever happened to me, this is where you must scrabble around in order to understand" were Serval's words to the Consul on handing him this typescript. For three days now I have been doing nothing but scrabbling, dabbling and paddling around in it.

The Crypt: it suggests a hidden meaning, a message encrypted. Somewhere in the book is a name, or a detail, or a *petit fait vrai*, or an invented one, a clue, or a colour, or a sign, or a cipher which refers to a secret in Serval's possession, a secret for the sake of which he may even have met his death. The fact that Serval asked the Consul to give the manuscript to me can only mean one thing – that it relates to something that took place in Grianta (since I know nothing about Serval's prior life in France or elsewhere, save that he was perhaps a pupil at Etampes for all or part of his secondary education), and that the affair involves one or more people sufficiently in the public eye for a mere maths teacher like me, ignorant as I am of the customs and culture of the expatriate community, to be able to spot it.

I've tried to identify everything in the book which might be thought to allude to Grianta. There aren't many allusions, but there are some.

Places

Gotterdam is nothing like Rotterdam, nor is it Copenhagen, Oslo or Helsinki; it doesn't resemble Montreal, Stockholm or Reykjavik. In fact, it's not really like anything at all, since the city is barely described. Serval mentions in passing a Royal Palace, a King William Square (with an equestrian statue in the middle), a St Margaret's Street, and "the sinister Binder Tower, where Groenjäger, the Bayard of Fernland, was incarcerated for five years." None of these has equivalents in Grianta. The President-for-Life has a fair number of palaces and residences, but they are all located far away from the town. He has had himself represented in effigy all over the place, but he hasn't yet had the gall to put his likeness on a horse. Grianta's modern prisons, built by West German specialists, equipped with the most sophisticated tools of non-destructive coercion, are masterpieces of contemporary custodial technology, and quite unlike the romantic Binder Tower or the monastic Marktendörin.

However, there are three places which play small roles in the plot invented by Serval which allude without doubt to Grianta.

The first is The Crest, easily recognised as the El Ghazâl. Both are luxury hotels nineteen floors high, dominating their respective cities, and both have the same "global clock" in their lobbies – a great planisphere showing the time in the main cities of the world, with internal lighting cunningly programmed to show where night and day fall.

The second is a restaurant, Matteotti's Pizzeria, "just next to the post office, opposite Gagliani's Italian delicatessen." That is where Serval meets the mysterious Monsieur Roussel, who must be someone fairly high up in the intelligence service. It has to be Mattei's restaurant, the one run by Gino, where, by the strangest coincidence, I happen to eat nearly all my meals. It is indeed beside the post office, and opposite Galignani's delicatessen.

The third is also a restaurant, located in Macrossan Street, "a quiet little street, not far from the Botanic Gardens and the main railway station." It is a French restaurant called La Bonne Chère: Blackstone takes Serval there, and tells him that it is the cover for the brothel where Anne Svendsen plies her trade, the brothel itself being called The Crypt. "'On the ground floor,' Blackstone explains, 'it's a perfectly respectable establishment, but in the lounges and private rooms upstairs the waitresses organise stupendous orgies; obviously, there's a hefty charge, which is why people here say that the name of the restaurant doesn't mean that the food is good (*la chère est bonne*) but that the maid comes dear (*la bonne est chère*)!'" (At this point, Serval the writer feels obliged to have Blackstone emit a "coarse guffaw.")

I suppose that Serval only used that name so as to have an excuse for inserting a hoary old French pun, but it also happens that Grianta's sole nightclub is located in Rue Saint-Marc (Saint-Marc, San Marco, Marco San, Macrossan . . .), a quiet side street not far from the Botanic Gardens and the railway station. It's called the Seven of Clubs, and last year it was the scene of a murky affair. The manageress, a buxom, good-looking woman who called herself Véronique de Grasse (she was from Alsace, and her real name was Grace Hillof), was found strangled by a necktie in one of her own bathrooms. The silk tie was pale blue and dotted with heraldic crests bearing lions or on ground sable crossed with azure – the arms of Blackbells Military Academy, Arizona, where five of the seventeen grandsons of the President-for-Life pretended to be cadets.

Is this then the story encrypted in *The Crypt*? It is tempting to think so (if only because of the book's title; but to my mind it's not the brothel's name which gave the book its title, but the book's title which determined the name of the brothel). On reflection, it won't hold water: there is no secret about the Seven of Clubs affair, only a self-preserving silence. Everyone knows who was responsible, but no one would dare to say it in public, and even less to write it down. The *English Mail*'s Grianta correspondent learned that the hard way. He implied in one of his stories that certain persons close to the President-for-Life were probably mixed up in it, and got kidnapped in broad daylight as he got out of a taxi in front of the Press Club. He's not been seen since. The international committee of enquiry which came to throw light on the affair conceded in the end that it had no jurisdiction. Some people say that the journalist is being kept alive one hundred kilometres from Grianta with his hands cut off, his eyes put out and his tongue torn off, but that is definitely an example of the black propaganda which the BH puts about to underpin its fearsome reputation.

Gotterdam's airport is called Hellige Luise, and Grianta's is at Saint Lucia. There is a similarity, but it's not really the same thing.

Names

Practically none of the names invented by Serval correspond to characters in Grianta. The nearest approximation is Roussel, the walk-on who lunches with Serval at Matteotti's Pizzeria and tells him of the "special training" which Vichard and Rouard had in earlier years. In Grianta, there is a Rousset who ostensibly runs a garage but whose real business, people say, is transferring the funds of local tycoons to accounts in Belgium and Switzerland.

One of the authors of the article on the "destructive effects of the CDP" is called Chappuis. The name perhaps comes from Serval's years at Etampes. There was a Chapuis (one p) at Etampes; in fact, there were two, "big" Chapuis and his "little" brother. The elder was called "Big Chapuis," the younger had a nickname that escapes me now. I don't know what became of them; at any rate, they're not in Grianta.

The facts

The history of Grianta is strewn with bloody deaths, unsolved enigmas, scandals quickly capped, with cases of blackmail, extortion, racketeering and foul deeds of every kind. The Seven of Clubs affair is alluded to only by a minor topographical detail; but there is another local scandal which is much more involved in the plot of *The Crypt*.

Six years ago, Grianta was selected as the site of the 1985 Pan-African Games. The government immediately decided to build a sports complex centred on a huge stadium with seating for one hundred thousand spectators. The cost was estimated at one hundred million dollars (and then some), and was to be financed by a loan from the International Monetary Fund, a subsidy from the Organisation for African Unity and from OPEC, a special tax, a national bond, and a lottery. The project leader was GICC, the Grianta Industrial Credit Corporation, a private bank in which the state held a minority interest, and whose managing director happened to be the brother-in-law of the President-for-Life. After protracted and tortuous dealings, the construction contract was awarded to the Italian firm of Balbi-Raversi.

Building work lasted three years. One month before the official opening, a crack appeared in one of the columns supporting the grand balcony, which collapsed and killed eleven site workers. There was a stage-managed trial which found two engineers and three foremen guilty. Everyone in Grianta knows what was really going on, but, once again, it was not something that anyone dared say in public.

This situation is reproduced point for point in the first part of *The Crypt*, where it serves to cast suspicion for a time on Einar Svendsen. The Fernland mogul is supposed to have won a contract to build a one-hundred-thousand-seat stadium for the VIIIth Nordic Sports Internationals. Construction was halted after eighteen months, when fraudulent workmanship was discovered in the foundations. The amount siphoned off by the contractors was said to come to two billion crowns. Svendsen clearly had loyal friends in government, because, not only was he not convicted, but also, a year later, when Mathias Henrijk based his novel *Öd Rädek* ("The Sinking") on the affair, Svendsen sued him for libel on the grounds that he was recognisably portrayed in the character of "Henry Swenson" – and won the case!

I have just reread these scrappy notes and I can see that I have been barking up the wrong tree. I have been trying in spite of myself to find a transparent allusion, a direct transcription. I'm going to find no such thing. Nothing narrated in this book – I mean, no part of the story explicitly told – could possibly be considered sufficiently compromising to have put Serval's life in danger. Yet vanish he did, after asserting that the truth was in this book. Is it a story from long ago, from somewhere else, about a character who has recently stepped into Grianta? What chance would I have of finding the trace of such a thing? I don't even know if anyone else has set eyes on this book, apart from the

Consul, who glanced through it without seeing anything (at any rate, he said nothing to me).

The truth is in these pages. It *must* be here. But where? Which of the myriad possible tracks will lead me towards it? I have that choking feeling as when faced with the crux of one of those logic problems where you can ask only one question to decide which of two men always tells the truth and which one only ever lies. But at the crossroads where I stand, there are not just two sentinels, but ten or fifteen of them, none of whom are perfectly consistent, abstract entities. One of them sometimes says what he believes to be true but can quite often be wrong; another says the opposite of what is put forward by a third, who talks rubbish anyway; a fourth man says something inaudible which is repeated by a fifth, who is known to be unreliable; a sixth claims to be a dissident Februarist to whom God has given the truth, which he will reveal only when February at last becomes a month of thirty days; a seventh obstinately refuses to say anything.

Does the missing page really matter? Or should I think: missing pages?

CHAPTER SIX

Search for a typist

Yesterday, Thursday, we heard that the curfew had been put back to midnight. Everyone had a ball. The cafés were packed once again, crowds sauntered under the eucalyptus trees on Cours de l'Indépendance, street orchestras sprang up spontaneously more or less everywhere; it was like a Ramadan night all over again. The patrols are less in evidence and less tense, at least in the town centre. But down in the docks and at Saint-Ferant skirmishing continues, apparently.

Yesterday evening I dined at Gino's with old Crozet. Everyone was there. Gino surpassed himself with his celebration *disinvoltura*, a velvety combination of four types of pasta, cooked separately but served together with elvers and red scallop-flesh: capelleti *alla sfondrata*, landriani in cream, fettucini *alla sorezana*, and Gino's latest creation, scagliolini "Bentivoglio," which are steamed in *contarini*, a local variety of truffle-flavoured seaweed which the Griantese adore. At the end of the meal, Gino fished a bottle of Friuli *grappa* out of his cellar, and we ended up bawling out old Italian ditties all together, with outrageous tremolos:

> Voi mi avete lasciatto
> Non siate ingiusto
> Verso di me, verso di me.
> Non lo merito
> Non lo merito   (repeat, ad lib)

However, before all that, Crozet had time to bring me up to date on Embassy gossip. Apparently the days of the Wazilah clan are numbered. The in-laws of the President-for-Life have lined their pockets much too handsomely, and the Beldi clique think that it's their turn now. It is not yet known whether Fahrid Beldi will become Prime Minister. He may prefer to remain at the Ministry of the Interior, where he can keep his eye on everything, and put one of his dummies, such as Boularkia, at the head of the government. The President-for-Life is supposed to have requested his lady wife to "watch where she puts her bum" (the actual words uttered by her noble spouse), and half a dozen Wazilahs may already have left the country. Needless to say, the heart does not bleed for them. The poorest, Jean-Ignace, who was a mere deputy director of the Department of Transport, when he needed a *pied à terre* in Paris, made do with a mansion at La Muette, for which he paid a trifling one and a half million pounds. On the French front, the Embassy and Consulate are, as always, sniping furiously at each other. The Ambassador has seized upon the Consul's absence in France to get him thrown off the executive committee of the Grianta French Residents' Association – simply by calling a general meeting and "forgetting" to send the notice to the Consul's supporters. Some of the latter turned up all the same, but there were too few of them to prevent the Ambassador from sweeping the board when it came to the vote. Crozet reckons the Consul will soon have nothing to twiddle but his thumbs, and will be lucky to stay chairman of the bridge club.

Crozet is priceless. He will certainly be very useful. But he's as leaky as a wet sponge, and I must be careful what I say. To my relief, it was he who brought up the Serval business, by asking me if I was in the know about the novelist's disappearance. I said I had heard talk of it at the Alliance Française.

"Just what I thought! There's been a rush on his books; I saw you borrowed three."

"Can't hide anything from you, that's for sure!"

"What do you think of them?"

I lied outrageously, saying I had not yet had time to read them.

"You can skip it, they're not worth a tinker's fart."

"Come on, now! A thriller writer who gets kidnapped is pretty exciting, isn't it?"

"Kidnapped? Pull the other one! You know what the police think? That he's swanned off with the wife of some bigwig, and that the whole thing is a front to protect him and his lady-love!"

"Don't you think the cover is over the top for that?"

Crozet shrugged his shoulders.

"You know, here, the weirder it is, the better it works. And it's worth going over the top to make sure you don't have the funny-men on your tail, if you see what I mean . . ."

I looked at Crozet, in disbelief. But all he did was smile, and place a finger over his lips.

I give Crozet's bizarre allusion only limited credence. To my mind, he knows nothing special, but, as usual, he likes to behave as if he knew a great deal. Anyway, whenever something slightly fishy happens here, people always say that the BH must be up to something.

As I reread Serval's typescript this morning for the umpteenth time, I suddenly became convinced that it was the work of a pro-fessional typist. It is just too clean and neat. If the writer had typed it out himself, he would have hesitated over something or other, or had second thoughts, or last-minute inspirations. Whereas this is flawless; it was manifestly typed by someone entirely outside of the book, seeking only to give a finished form to something which must have previously been a tangled mess of inky pages, with a whole system of deletions, insertions, arrows, marginalia, carets, asterisks and intercalations to mark the path to the envis-aged final product.

The idea plunged me into a state of feverish excitement. Not so much because the typist might have kept a trace of the last pages of the manuscript, but because of the earlier states of the text. If the novel really held a secret, then there could be no doubt, in my mind, that a study of the drafts would reveal most of the keys and show (for example) how this or that name had been chosen, or which real event was transposed in this or that twist of Serval's tale.

I devoted the whole day to looking for the typist. That would not have been an arduous task in itself, but I was not keen to inform all Grianta that I had in my hands the latest (or the last book by the misanthropic novelist who called himself Serval.

It was clear that Serval would not have entrusted the typing of a text containing explosive revelations (even if only cryptically) to anyone in whom he did not have complete faith, or who did not work in circumstances allowing the necessary discretion. That would rule out all the secretaries at the consulate and the embassy, for example, who happily filled their desk hours with endless little jobs on the side. For the same reason it was unlikely that Serval had had recourse to the El Ghazâl's typing pool, whose members, I have heard it said, could more properly be referred to as hotel secs. It's only on the brochure that they look effective and functional anyway.

Then there were three or four secretarial agencies in town, and the fifteen or so freelance typists listed in the yellow pages. I was preparing to call them one by one with a different convoluted fib for each, when I had a better idea. I went to see the manager of the printing firm I had been in touch with at the time of the Grianta exhibition and fair. I showed him a couple of sheets of the typescript and asked him if he could say what kind of typewriter had been used.

Without a moment's hesitation he said that it was an Olivetti Lexicon 80E:

"One of the very first electric typewriters. When you press line-return, it's like firing a recoilless 75mm mortar. In other respects, it's indestructible – a typewriter built like a tank!"

By a splendid stroke of luck, I happen to know the Olivetti agent in Grianta very well. He's called Colomb. I play bridge with him twice a week. He's a man of great discretion and an unusually nice man too, in the small world of swanks and loudmouths who make up the expatriate French community here. He can pull off a double-bluff *schlemm* like no other, and always seems genuinely sorry to have known which way to finesse.

I went to see him towards the end of the afternoon. He was unpacking recent models that had just arrived from Europe – magical machines with line memories, multiple fonts, corrector ribbons, and heaps of advanced and ultra-sophisticated features. When I mentioned the Lexicon 80E to him, he began to laugh.

"But they must have stopped making those things fifteen years ago . . ."

"I'm sure there are some still in use here. Apparently they go on for ever . . . "

"They're sturdy, that's true, but they're close to being antiques . . . What do you want to know, exactly?"

I explained that I was looking for a typist who still used an Olivetti Lexicon 80E.

"I've still got some under maintenance contracts. Mainly in offices. Anyway, let's have a look . . . "

He opened a metal box, pulled out a small stack of record cards, and flicked through them.

A minute later I had what I was looking for: the name and address of Mademoiselle Lise Carpenter, 38 Avenue des Glycines, at La Crique.

CHAPTER SEVEN

Lise Carpenter

Today's report ought to consist of tiny, insignificant details. And yet I feel that my enquiry is making fundamental progress.

I spent the whole morning thinking, and then decided to go and see Mademoiselle Carpenter without making an appointment in advance. Obviously, I would have to tell her the whole truth, that is to say, I would have to divulge the mission that the Consul had entrusted to me, and I preferred not to have to do so on the telephone. I know that all these things, seen from the outside, must look like symptoms of persecution mania or acute conspirationitis. But the danger is real. As far as I know, no one else yet has an inkling of the existence of this manuscript, and it's much better that way.

La Crique is one of Grianta's fashionable beach resorts. The area is a little less expensive and classy than Cap-Blanc, Corchney, Chekina or Les Pêcheurs, but it's still pretty well restricted to MDs, international officials, and the *jeunesse dorée*, which flocks to a ghastly discotheque called The Pit and the Pendulum.

I found Avenue des Glycines – "Wisteria Drive" – with no trouble. It is a private road lined, in spite of its name, with magnolias, and it serves neocolonial bungalows nestling behind thickets of bougainvillaea and hibiscus. Amongst these rather flashy dwellings, number 38 is conspicuously plain. It is a tiny, one-story house; almost a doll's house, so to speak.

I rang, and wondered what the person who would come to the door would look like. Would she be an English old maid (because of the name, Carpenter)? Or a peroxide blonde in a miniskirt and a barely buttoned blouse? I was taken aback when a wispy girl with very black hair, almond eyes, and high, salient cheekbones appeared on the doorstep—not only because she was not at all like the picture I had just been painting in my mind, but because I knew her. In recent weeks, I have seen her often at Galignani's, where she buys ham and cheese, just as I do. We had even said hello to each other, though without ever getting into conversation.

I saw by her glance that she also recognised me. That ought to have made the introduction easier, but in fact it threw me completely, and I began bumbling. When I got to mentioning the name of Serval, her smile vanished and her face clouded over.

"Are you from the police?"

I shook my head hard, and put out an arm to stop her from closing the door on me. I explained in a jerky and hesitant voice that I was just a maths teacher at the Lycée Français with the same tastes as she had for San Daniele and Parmesan cheese, thrust in spite of himself into a quite incomprehensible affair. I must have sounded so bleating and dim that in the end she took pity and let me in, asked me to sit down, and to tell her the whole story, calmly.

I recovered my wits, more or less. I gave Lise Carpenter a precise résumé, repeating everything that the Consul had told me about Serval, telling her about my reading of *The Crypt*, and sharing with her the various hypotheses that I had built on it. I told her that in order to test out any of them I would need access to the very last pages of the book and especially to earlier drafts of it.

Mademoiselle Carpenter shook her head. She had never had the drafts. Serval used to come every day to dictate two or three pages to her. His "first drafts" consisted of an inextricable tangle of notes scrawled in every direction on the pages of a spiral notepad of the sort used by shorthand typists. He seemed to know how to find his way around his notes and, though he dictated slowly, he spoke with complete firmness, without erring or umming or having second thoughts. When he had finished with a page of his pad, he would tear it out, fold it in two lengthwise and pull it through the slit of a parallelepipedic metal and plexiglass box, much the same size as a paperback book, which turned the page into confetti. He seemed to attach great importance to the shredding operation.

There was no last page, either. "As far as I'm concerned, that's it," he had told Mademoiselle Carpenter. "After the explanation, doubt. My readers are beginning to get the hang, and have learned to read between the lines, and beyond them. If the publisher really insists, maybe I'll cross the tees for him, but it would be a shame."

Mademoiselle Carpenter had wanted to know whether a tee-crossing dénouement would expose only Vichard, or whether it would also pin something on to the other three – Barrett, Svendsen and his daughter Anne – who had never been completely cleared of suspicion.

"Everyone expects it to be a diabolical plot set up by Vichard. But you could go one better, not with Barrett or Svendsen, who wouldn't be interesting culprits since they've had too much suspicion cast on them already, but with Anne. She's a highly intelligent girl, close to all the main characters in the drama; she could very well have pulled all the strings from the start. To convince my readers of that at the very end would be a much more brilliant pirouette to pull off than simply turning the false suspect who has been cleared back into the real culprit again."

Then I asked Lise Carpenter if Serval's behaviour had altered over recent weeks. She thought for a few moments before answering:

"Obviously, in the light of what you have just told me, I could claim to have noticed that he was edgy and ill at ease; but to be honest, I can only see that now, in retrospect. Once or twice he got here very late, whereas he was normally as punctual as a prince. Another time, he brought back a page that I had typed more than a week previously, and asked me to do it again. I don't know if that's at all connected with what concerns you, but it amazed me, it really did."

"What, in particular, was on that page?"

"Nothing, apparently, apart from a name he wanted to change, the name of Svendsen's yacht."

"*Monitor*?"

"Yes, *Monitor*. Before, it was called *Misène*."

"But the yacht plays no part in the plot, anyway!"

"I know! I told him I could easily white out *Misène* and type in *Monitor*, that the correction would be invisible, and would be much quicker. But he insisted on my retyping the whole page . . . "

After a moment's silence, Lise Carpenter went on:

"I think I can be of some use to you all the same. Before start-ing to dictate his book to me, Serval told me the story and said what his models and sources were. I remember it because it was very funny, like a master-class in literary fiddling: 'Please, dear Miss, don't think that I make things up. All I do is purloin var-ious details from here and from there so as to connect my own story up. Everyone does it that way – and I don't just mean crime writers! Look at Antoine Berthet! or Bovary! Three quarters of Balzac come from news items, and when it's not the real or half-real world which inspires a writer, then it's someone else's fiction, or for want of anything better, one of his own books. Do you know how many *Don Carloses* have been written? Not far short of fifty! And there is one that begins with this entirely unambig-uous warning:

"'This story is drawn from Spanish, French, Italian and Flem-ish authors who have written about the period in which it is set. The principal amongst them are M de Thou, Aubigné, Brantôme, Cabrera, Adriana, Natalis Comes, Dupleix, Mathieu, Mayerne, Mézeray, Le Laboureur sur Castelnau, Strada, Meteren, the histo-rian of Don Juan of Austria, the eulogies of Father Hilarion da Costa, a Spanish book on the words and deeds of Philip II, an account of the death and burial of his son, etc. It is also drawn from manuscript and printed sources pertaining to the story, including a little book in verse entitled *Diogenes*, which deals with it exhaustively, and a manuscript by M de Peiresc directly on the same subject.'"

So there were four models used in different ways for the plot, or rather plots, of *The Crypt*. What that means for me in particular is that the secret that I am trying to grasp is not lurking in any of the specifically detective aspects of the book, but in a detail, perhaps a superfluous one (like the transformation of *Misène* into *Monitor*, which remains an insoluble brain-teaser . . .).

The first model comes from Agatha Christie's *And Then There Were None*. As is well known, nine unconvicted culprits are exe-cuted in this book by a judge who makes it seem as if he is the tenth (but not the last) victim. The magistrate-murderer is called

Lawrence Wargrave, which is indeed the name Serval has given to the author of *The Magistrate is the Murderer*.

The second model had been "dropped in mid-stream," but Serval made a point of mentioning it all the same. It was a short story by Maurice Leblanc, part of the Arsène Lupin cycle, entitled *Swan-Neck Edith*. In this story, Colonel Sparmiento is supposed to have committed suicide after having been robbed of his twelve tapestries (of the Bayeux variety). The Edith of the title identifies "the body of a horribly mutilated man whose face no longer had any human features" as her husband's corpse. In fact, it is all an insurance fiddle, for Sparmiento = Lupin, and the corpse, the body of a person unknown, was stolen from the morgue at Lille.

The third provides the whole basis for Wargrave's pseudo-novel, which Serval himself declared, is no more than a feeble rehash of it. It is an unjustly forgotten novel by a good writer of the 1950s, Bill Ballinger, entitled *The Tooth and the Nail*, which recounts how a young conjuror tracks down the counterfeiter who had murdered his wife and got away with it, gets taken on as the culprit's chauffeur, and cooks up his own demise with dazzling brilliance.

The fourth source is certainly the one which puzzles me the most. It consists of fourteen lines from a novel which Serval brought that day to Mademoiselle Carpenter, and asked her to copy out. He had changed some words – twelve words, to be precise, crossed out in black felt-tip, and replaced by twelve others inserted in tiny handwriting above the line.

Lise Carpenter kept the book, so she went to fetch it from her room and then gave it to me. It is called *The Koala Case Mystery*.

"A spy story," she said. "Not a very good one."

I put off studying the fourteen lines and the book until later. Mademoiselle Carpenter offered me iced tea. One thing leads to another and I asked her out to dinner. I had wanted to do so ever since the start of our conversation. She accepted very spontaneously. When I asked her if she had a favourite place, she replied that she had wanted for ages to go to The Bust of Tiberius. I would rather have dined at Gino's, where I have my habits, but I agreed, eagerly.

We met at the small café downstairs at the Alliance Française, and went out on the Trecurzah road.

The Bust of Tiberius was jampacked, as it always is; fortunately, I had remembered to telephone ahead. We made our way around the tables with frozen half-smiles on our faces, acknowledging acquaintances, of whom there was, God knows, a whole heap, from the editor of *En Avant!* to the Ambassador's wife, from the principal of the military academy to the local golf champion.

I must admit that what we were served this evening– sea squirt and braised tuna fish *en gelée* – was delicious. But I still maintain that The Bust of Tiberius is a restaurant less remarkable for its food than for its position. As it stands right on top of the site, it has one of the most staggering panoramic views in the world, and it is a terrible pity that the unforgettable experience of first setting eyes on one of the best preserved cities of the Ancient World is utterly ruined from October to March by the *son et lumière* which one or another of the Wazilahs has wangled out of UNESCO, and which nets him a clear $100,000 a year. And even in the low season, you are often prevented from marvelling in peace by swarms of ragamuffins who latch on to tourists and visitors, trying to trade forged drachmas, silver fish pendants and mock oil lamps. But this evening, perhaps because it is midweek, or because Lise Carpenter turned out to be a marvellous dinner partner, it was quite simply sublime.

CHAPTER EIGHT

The Koala Case Mystery

"So less than a month after arriving at Newcastle, Blanes found himself Head of the Department of Theoretical Physics.

"His office was quite unlike an ordinary scientist's place of work. His muddle and inconsistency made him a typical laid-back American intellectual. On his desktops and on his shelves were few physics textbooks and barely a handful of theses and journals. There were no graphs or flowcharts on the walls, but a big reproduction (amongst others) of Brighella's *Lamentations of Job*, onto which a Jobcentre flier had been gummed. The cleaning ladies had long since given up trying, but if you rummaged around in this glory-hole, you might come across, higgledy-piggledy, a calligrapher's handbook, an FA cup rosette, the complete works of Sacher-Masoch in a shiny simulation leather binding, a toy mortar barrel, or an old issue of the *New York Times*. You could imagine that the room had been arranged like that as part of an exorbitantly wilful plan of disorganisation, as if it had to look like a crafty, artful construction and not at all like the den of a man in search of secret truths. You would have expected a microscope or a pair of scales or a typewriter, but what you found instead was a photograph of a woman winning the hundred-metre event, or of the palace at Hampton Court. In this cunningly randomised tip, you could dearly guess the fearful effort that had gone into creating an appearance of casual niceness. Did Blanes really need a poster of majorettes in action at Fort-de-France to stimulate his brain cells – or was it there to disconcert his visitors?"

In Serval's book, the description of Blackstone's office is closely based on this passage, even though it differs at the very beginning from the letter if not from the spirit of the original text:

"Detective Inspector Blackstone was reputedly eccentric because his office was quite unlike an ordinary policeman's place of work. It was a laid-back, muddly mess. There were no weighty tomes of criminology, no archives, no map of Gotterdam dotted with colour-coded pins, but, for example, on the wall, a large reproduction of Brighella's *Benedictions of Job*, onto which a Jobcentre flier had been gummed. The cleaning ladies had long since given up trying, but if you rummaged around in this glory-hole, you might come across, higgledy-piggledy, a pencraftsman's handbook, a kaleidoscope, the complete works of Carlo Frugoni in a shiny simulation leather binding, a toy De Dion-Bouton, or an old issue of *Smith's Weekly*. You could imagine that the room had been arranged like that, as part of a too evidently wilful plan of disorganisation, as if it had to look like a stupid, futile construction and not at all like the den of a man in search of secret truths. You would have expected a microscope or a pair of scales or a typewriter, but what you found instead was a photograph of a woman winning the trampolining event, or of a palace in Tripolitania. In this cunningly randomised tip, you could almost intuit the fearful effort that had gone into creating an appearance of casual niceness. Did Blackstone really need a poster of majorettes in action at North Detroit to stimulate his brain cells – or was it there to disconcert his visitors?"

From "a large reproduction" to "his visitors," the two passages are identical save for twelve words, twelve twelve-letter words replaced by twelve other twelve-letter words (not counting the tiny grammatical changes that they involve, nor the change of the character's name):

LAMENTATIONS	BENEDICTIONS
CALLIGRAPHER	PENCRAFTSMAN
FACUPROSETTE	KALEIDOSCOPE
SACHERMASOCH	CARLOFRUGONI
MORTARBARREL	DEDIONBOUTON
NEWYORKTIMES	SMITHSWEEKLY
EXORBITANTLY	TOOEVIDENTLY
CRAFTYARTFUL	STUPIDFUTILE
HUNDREDMETRE	TRAMPOLINING
HAMPTONCOURT	TRIPOLITANIA
CLEARLYGUESS	ALMOSTINTUIT
FORTDEFRANCE	NORTHDETROIT

I spent ages studying this pair of lists, but I didn't glean anything at all from the comparison. Both for relaxation and in the hope of picking up further clues, I read the novel from which Serval had made Lise retype this half-page.

At an international astronautics congress in Milan, an American physicist by the name of William Vidornaught is contacted by a French colleague, Henri Legros, who makes an appointment to meet him that same evening in a big café in the Vittorio-Emanuele arcade. When Vidornaught gets to the café he finds Legros already there, sitting at a little low table at the very back, talking to someone else. They seem to be talking heatedly. Suddenly, just as Vidornaught reaches the table, the other man stands up, bawls out "OK, so you can have your cut!" and plunges a knife into Legros, who falls to the floor. The stranger runs off. The café erupts in panic. Vidornaught rushes to the side of Legros, who just has time to whisper "Macklin in London" before he expires. When Vidornaught stands up, he realises that his hands are covered in blood; customers have formed a horrified circle around him, and he grasps that they take him to be the murderer. His first reflex is to bolt for the back door. Meanwhile, a dozen *carabinieri* have appeared at the front.

Next morning, his photograph is displayed on the front pages of all the papers. Vidornaught takes refuge with the only friend he has in Italy, an optician in Menaggio, called Alesi. Vidornaught manages to obtain false identity papers, with which he flees to England.

But he has scarcely stepped onto the platform at Waterloo when two men accost him, one on each side, then drag him off and push him into a fast car which is soon roaring through the English countryside. That is where the deal is put on the table: either he agrees to collaborate, or he will be handed over to the police.

Who are these men? Two KGB agents, called (or purporting to be called) Soltykov and Apraksin.

What do they want? The Koala Code.

Why should Vidornaught be likely to supply them with a code he has never heard of before?

The answer to this last question occupies a good third of the whole book, and takes the reader on a whirling and somewhat tiresome roundabout of double agents, spies who come in from the cold, men who know too much, comrades called X and bulldogs at bay, with rapid shifts of scenery from Tunis to Algiers, Paris, Ankara, Exeter, Chile and Indonesia. After reading the book if not diagonally then at least on a rhumb, it is not humanly possible to give an intelligible plot summary. The best you can hope for is an explanation of where things are at when the KGB have cornered Vidornaught, and of what's at the bottom of it all.

The Koala Code takes the physical form of a slim tome entitled *A Grammar of the Malayan Language* by W. Marsden. All American agents serving in southeast Asia and Oceania have a copy. It enables them

a) to identify at a glance the code and cover names of all and any of their honourable correspondents and team mates from the Maldives to the Marquesas

b) to send or receive within thirty minutes any message of up to eight thousand characters and spaces

c) to establish their geographical bearings to an accuracy of the order of one second of one degree.

The KGB have several copies of the Koala Code in their possession, of course, which have given those of its members previously unfamiliar with Malayalam the opportunity to learn the rudiments of its grammar, but nothing else. The KGB also know that the key to the Koala Code is located at an intelligence base at Newcastle, in New Zealand. It is the CIA's Oceania HQ, and also a radio navigation post for spy satellites, a space module recovery base and an astronautics lab. A KGB man has managed to infiltrate it– a computer scientist called Shepherd (real name Baralshin), but you can't rule out the possibility that the aforementioned Shepherd has *gone over*; at least, that's what a Sri Lankan stringer called Hang Puah implies before he vanishes.

The KGB would like to lay its hands on Hang Puah (if he still exists), to acquire proof of Shepherd's treachery, and to obtain, not the Koala Code key, but a large enough sample of messages for the Kremlin number crunchers to crack the cipher.

A physicist called Blanes, first name Abraham (Abe to his

friends), is soon to be sent to the Newcastle astronautics laboratory. Vidornaught looks near enough like Blanes for minimal
plastic surgery to make him a passable double (this is one of the
book's *very* weak points; but we'll let it pass . . .). The KGB's idea
is to kidnap Blanes when he stops over at Changhi airport and to
put Vidornaught in his place.

For reasons that have more to do with the needs of the book
than with the real world (for even if every police force in the globe
were after him, he could easily demonstrate that he was not guilty
of the murder of Legros), Vidornaught accepts the mission. Suit-
ably transmogrified and briefed, he takes Blanes's place and turns
up at Newcastle. Of course, he has barely settled in when he blows
the KGB's plot to the laboratory director, who is called Barrett,
just like the "ugly American" of *The Crypt*.

The trouble is that Barrett does not believe him, or rather, pretends not to (it's rather contorted, you'll soon see why). However,
Shepherd gets to hear of it. Now Shepherd has not *gone over* at all –
he is only a *false* double agent. Upon which, Vidornaught-Blanes's
little number seems to be up, and all the more so when the "real"
Blanes, allegedly shot dead by Apraksin (a bullet in the neck) in
the transit lounge toilets at Changhi, reappears, since Apraksin
is a *genuine* double agent. Various episodes follow, involving
plastic vats in fusion, pools patrolled by piranhas, alligators and
man-eating eels, knife-throwers, bare-handed brick splitters, fake
beggars, inscrutably smiling oriental gentlemen, space shuttles
exploding in midflight and luscious Eurasian girls with ao-dais
that open up to *there*. Just how Vidornaught succeeds in escaping
from Hang Puah's clutches, to eliminate Shepherd-Baralshin, to
save Blanes from a horrible death, to unmask Barrett (who had
set up the entire operation just to get rid of Soltykov), to prove
his innocence, and, on the side, as it were, to win fair Charlotte
Knabelhuber, the NASA laboratory boss, is explained in the last
thirty pages of the book.

As long as you don't get too hooked on the details, it's quite
readable. The ending is even quite lively. The author is good on
local colour, on descriptions and dialogue, but his explanations
are not terribly clear, to put it mildly, and he sets enigmas without

taking the trouble to solve them first. For instance, we will never know why Vidornaught was contacted by Legros; nor why the former agrees to the meeting. Who is this "Macklin in London"? How can he hope to find Macklin without knowing his first name, his profession or his address? It is obvious that if Vidornaught had thought for a second, then he would have stopped behaving like the murderer which he was not, and would have gone straight to the police. But in that case, there would have been no book . . .

All in all, though, it is no more far-fetched than any of the ten or fifteen spy stories I read in a year.

My problem is obviously different. Neither the book as a whole, nor the twelve changes made by Serval to the paragraph which he borrowed from it for his own book, shed any light on anything at all.

Maybe Grianta was the scene of bloody score-settling between spies from different camps; there's no doubt that the CIA, the KGB and half a dozen other intelligence services have active networks here, if only because of the uranium at Bab el-Zghal and San Casilda, or for the sake of the Crubelier archipelago, of ever increasing strategic importance. But why should Serval be mixed up in those kinds of stories? In any case, a secret is supposed to be hidden in *The Crypt*, not in the *Koala Case Mystery* . . .

CHAPTER NINE

The Black Hand

I found it hard to get to sleep, and when I did, my sleep was troubled by dreams, perhaps by portents of the future.

All morning, an inexplicable intuition has been nagging at my mind: that the truth I am after is not *in* the book, but *between* the books. That may sound senseless, but I know what I mean: that you have to read the *differences*, you have to read between the books, in the way you read "between the lines." For there is not just a book-or rather, a typescript-called *The Crypt*, there are the four books used to greater or lesser extent by Serval to write it. Inside *The Crypt* itself, there is *The Magistrate is the Murderer*, and also, although it is only mentioned in half a sentence, Henrijk's novel, *Öd Rädek*. Odd things shift and slip from one text to another, sometimes intact, sometimes with minute alterations. The exemplar of all these changes, the instance which makes you think about all the others and suspect that they have an important function in the construction of Serval's book, is, obviously, the set of twelve words from the passage taken over from *The Koala Case Mystery*. But you can find more every time you open the book. For instance, Mattei's restaurant becomes Matteotti's, Henrijk's Henry Swenson becomes Einar Svendsen, the Rousset of Grianta is perhaps the original of Roussel, and the Etampes Chapuis the source of Chappuis; Vidornaught becomes Blanes in *The Koala Case Mystery*, and in *The Crypt* he becomes Blackstone (at least, he lends him his office, save for twelve words), *Misène* becomes *Monitor*, the Barrett from *The Koala Case* gives his name to the Barrett of *The Crypt*, Lawrence Wargrave, a character in a novel by Agatha Christie, becomes the fictional author of *The Magistrate is the Murderer*. The Seven of Clubs becomes The Crypt, which is itself hidden behind the name of La Bonne Chère (not to mention that "La bonne chère," "good food," becomes *la bonne chère*, "the expensive maid"), and so on.

The book's secret lies neither in the anecdotes it narrates nor in its plot, but in the twists that it makes to these names, and to many others I could mention.

The idea takes hold of me, goes round and round in my head, and convinces me that I have a lead. The lead that I have found fills me with dread.

Not all the name changes are of equal weight. Spilling the beans on the fiddles perpetrated by a Svendsen by calling him Swenson, or using the name of a school friend for a secondary character, do not bear on the course of the story in the same way as, for example, moving a major character from one book to another. I have come to the conclusion that only three of these alterations are really significant, I mean, were made knowingly, and to attract attention to themselves: first, those which connect *The Koala Case Mystery* to *The Crypt*, namely the character called Vidornaught-Blanes, who becomes Blackstone, and the Barrett who is common to both books (connecting them like a bar or axle, *barrette* in French); then the metamorphosis of *Misène* into *Monitor*, which is irrelevant to the plot but obviously crucial for Serval.

I jotted down the three pairings, as I would have laid out an equation:

$$VID\ (BLA) \longrightarrow BLA$$
$$BAR \longrightarrow BAR$$
$$MO \longrightarrow Ml$$

Blabla, Babar, Barmy – some of the conjunctions look almost like jokes; but the smile froze on my face when I read the right-hand column from top to bottom. For if there is one name that no one in Grianta pronounces without a shiver of fear, it is that of Alphonse Blabami, head man of the Black Hand!

I flatter myself that I am a being endowed with the gift of reason. I am well aware how easily an idée fixe can plunge you into vapid fantasy, and I know that anagrams and logogriphs have a thrill all their own. By definition, the twenty-six letters of the alphabet can be made to mean anything you want. The Black Hand has come to mind, more or less vaguely, several times already in connection with Serval's disappearance; and Crozet actually alluded to it in my presence. To begin with, I preferred to believe that I was letting myself slip into the collective paranoia which the Black Hand aims to instil in us all. However, the discovery of this tortuously encrypted name rang such specific bells in my mind that I reread particular passages of *The Crypt* with great care, and I can confirm that my intuition was not wrong: Serval really was thinking of that despicable torturer when he wrote his book.

Why had I not spotted it sooner, unless I was instinctively shying away from a track which leads to fearsome danger? Blabami is the spitting image of Fly – who had served in the Marines, had been a professional wrestler, is aged about fifty, is completely bald, and has a broken nose.

Blabami doesn't have a broken nose, but he is completely bald; he served in Indochina as a sergeant in a French colonial regiment; he hasn't been a wrestler, but won medals for weightlifting; like Fly, he drives a white Mercedes.

He lives in a huge villa which has all the trappings of a fortress, at Les Pêcheurs, a little port about twenty kilometres north of Grianta (just as Vichard and Rouard live in a huge villa at Flåksund, a small fishing port twenty kilometres outside Gotterdam). He has a mistress called Martine, just like the name of the adapted version (another "version"!) of the Arethusa 234F MTB, whose stage name, Martine Fontaine, explains Arethusa (the spring of Arethusa is "la *fontaine* d'Aréthuse"). And she is the star – in French, *vedette*, which also means "torpedo boat" – of a television show.

These resemblances cannot all be counted as coincidental. I have no clue why these allusions are made; maybe the key is hidden in the twelve twelve-letter words; but I still haven't got anywhere with them.

The Black Hand rose to notoriety in the late 1950s when the current President-for-Life, at the time a practising lawyer, founded the PIP, the People's Independence Party. In the 1959 elections the PIP won thirty-five per cent of the seats in the local Representative Assembly, ninety-five per cent of which had always been held by colonial stooges. Eager to stem the rising tide of independence as rapidly as possible, the French government, with its habitual clumsiness, promulgated a series of reforms which were judged inadequate by the nationalists, and far too generous by the settlers. Riots, probably instigated by *agents provocateurs*, broke out at Cularo and Ghita and provided a pretext for bloody repression. The President-for-Life was deported to the Crubelier Islands (whence his title of "Supreme Martyr," by which radio and television announcers still refer to him), the PIP and the trade unions were dissolved and all newspapers were banned. Over the following months the Black Hand, with army and police protection (and on occasion with their active assistance), murdered several dozen if not several hundred supporters of the PIP and the GAW (General Association of Workers). The announcement of the first secret talks held in the Comores between France and members of the central committee of the underground PIP prompted a new wave of violent incidents, some of which were outright slaughter – such as the events of 10 June 1961, when two score of the Black Hand's gangsters massacred the entire population of six hundred and forty-three men, women and children of the village of Ourglane, in the heart of the mining area.

On the proclamation of independence on 5 May 1962 only three of the leaders of the Black Hand left the country: Dr Allard-Duplantier, Lussinge, and the civil engineering contractor, Monnier. Once it was established that French interests (the interests of France, that is, as well as the interests of French settlers) would not be touched, that Grianta would remain within the sphere of French economic and political influence, the Black Hand agreed to collaborate with the President-for-Life, who had great need of a parallel police force both in order to maintain his position within the PIP (the murder of Dieudonné Affo at Darmstadt) and to wage war on the left-wing opposition which persisted in the fond belief that independence and democracy could go hand in hand. The Black Hand very soon became a tool of repression in the pay of the cliques which held power. It now recruited tough guys not just amongst poor whites but from the native population too. Blabami joined in 1963, people say, and scaled every rung of its secret ladder to become supreme leader in 1972.

The structures and methods of the BH are borrowed from various secret societies – the Sicilian mafia, the Camorra in Naples, the Doriani of Bari, the Fiscalrassi of Montenegro. Its members are called *mortaretti* – an Italian word (there have always been significant Italian and Maltese minorities in Grianta) originally meaning "a small mortar," but which actually refers to the sawn-off shotguns which most BH members use. They generally act in groups of five, called a "hand": four "fingers" and a leader, the "thumb"; four "thumbs" are led by a "number one thumb," four "number one thumbs" are under a "big thumb." Above big-thumb level, the organisation awards sonorous titles to those who are near to the apex of the pyramid – "knight," "commander," "first master," "master," "grandmaster." The dreadful reputation for cruelty which they enjoy is by no means a mere figment of the popular imagination. Almost everyone in Grianta has had at least one opportunity to see what the BH can do. On some days, you find men impaled on the railings of the Botanic Gardens; on others, you see them hanging by their guts from the plane trees in Place des Trophées. When the BH condemn a man to death for some reason or other they often also exterminate the whole family, and sometimes do for his friends and neighbours too. They mutilate their victims in viciously symbolic ways. A girl who saw something she shouldn't have seen may have her eyes ripped out and stitched into the palm of her right hand; a man may be made to eat his own testicles; someone who tried to help a man the BH were after might have his hands and his feet cut off.

At the beginning, the BH was an exclusively political organisation. It was the praetorian guard, the ragtag collection of *tonton macoutes* who settled scores with anyone who tried to obstruct the rise and rise of the President-for-Life. They dealt first with the other leaders of the PIP, the "Historic Leaders of the National Revolution," and eliminated them one by one. Then when the President-for-Life had assumed personal and absolute power over all legislative, executive and judicial matters, the Black Hand turned its attention to those whose mere existence could be construed as potential opposition – students, judges, journalists, workers' representatives on company boards, etc. There was a bloody purge of the entire class of cadres, including senior police and army officers holding views that were not exactly liberal, in the sole interest of the Mnasteri clan and its Wazilah, Beldi and Oumboulélé connections. During the disturbances in 1968, Black Hand men went into hospital wards to finish off wounded demonstrators. Over thirty doctors and nurses were savagely murdered for giving first aid to "red dogs."

However, since those days the Black Hand has progressively turned itself into a state within the state. It is quite outside the control of those whom it is supposed to serve, and, in the absence of institutional or legal structures to limit its role, it has taken to intervening in public and private affairs. At first it permitted the ruling clique to dip gaily into the nation's coffers, then, seeing that there was nothing to hold it back, decided to set itself up in the same line of business, so to speak. It began with the Fisheries Board, then went on to licensing stalls at the central market, and expanded into passports, emigration, the law society, etc. At the present time the BH runs a racket in practically every branch of life in the country: it fixes the price of wheat, cooking oil and fish, it takes a percentage on all goods entering and leaving the country, and it levies hefty charges on traders to protect them from its own thugs. Civil engineering, road works, port facilities, travel agencies, the land registry, sports clubs, cinemas, the Tourist Board, and coach hire firms are all in its grip, as are most offices of the state. Its whim makes and unmakes careers in government service, in banks, in ministries and, in the last analysis, the President-for-Life is less the master of the BH than its catspaw.

People say that there are some poor whites left in the BH and, at the top of the hierarchy, two or three former settler bosses who have resurfaced as technical advisers to keep an eye on the interests which Paris has not only managed to retain in its former colony but has expanded quite substantially. But broadly speaking Europeans are not involved with the BH. The case of the *English Mail* correspondent was extremely unusual; *a priori*, it would be almost unthinkable if Serval had provoked the wrath of the Black Hand. Even if there were a grain of truth in what Crozet insinuated, namely that Serval had had an affair with the wife (or mistress) of a bigwig in the government (or in the BH itself), I can't see, unless of course I have *not read properly*, unless I have got it wrong from start to finish, what "truth" about that affair might have been smuggled into the typescript.

Nonetheless the Black Hand's presence in this book is real. It is not just a figment of my imagination or the product of coincidences. But it is not – and this is fundamental, I think – it is not directly discernible from a reading of *The Crypt* on its own. It was only when Lise put me on to *The Koala Case Mystery* and showed me the page retyped solely in order to alter the otherwise insignificant name of a yacht that I had an inkling of the presence of the BH or could check out the intuition and turn it into a conviction. Without those two leads there would have been no marker at all to tell me that the BLA of Blackstone (and Blanes), the BA of Barrett and the MI of Misène had a special status; and even supposing that the name of the "Arethusa 234F code-name Martine" had made me "think" of Blabami's callipygian doxy, I would have been naturally inclined to see in it only one of the private jokes which constitute the lifeblood of the French community in Grianta.

The "truth" which I seek is encrypted not just in the book on its own, but also in the circumstances of its composition. The clues are no doubt contained in the facts of the story, in the names, in the psychological and criminal motives of the characters, and in the descriptions of places and of people, but they are also contained in the way the manuscript was typed, in the books which inspired the author to a greater or lesser extent, and in the pastiches, textual cocktails and outright borrowings in which he has indulged.

That is exactly what Serval would have told me if he could have done so, as he told the Consul he would, by "getting in touch with me directly to give all necessary instructions." But he could just as easily have forewarned the Consul; he could have given him a copy of *The Koala Case Mystery* together with his own typescript, or told him to see Lise for additional information. BUT THAT IS JUST WHAT HE DID *NOT* DO! Does that mean that he did not trust the Consul?

CHAPTER TEN

Mind in a whirl

I'll be killed if I don't scarper: didn't Serval say something like that to the Consul? So the threat is clearly located here, in Grianta; and here, if you have anything to do with the BH, you're just as clearly under threat.

I am afraid. I don't really know why, nor do I really know what it is that I am afraid of. Obviously I don't dare talk about it to Crozet or to anyone at the Embassy. I have the feeling that there are wheels within wheels which are being kept hidden from me. Am I being manipulated behind my back? But how? And for what reason?

At eleven this morning, I ended up telephoning Lise. I think she is the only person in Grianta who might be able to help.

She was about to go out for a swim at Chekina, and she suggested I join her there. Since she would have to drive across the city to get there, I said she might as well pick me up on the way. Half an hour later she turned up at the wheel of a minimoke adorned with an orange tent-canvas sunshade. She wore one of those printed cotton pareos which the bratpack at the Club have made a must. Her shoulders were the colour of honey.

En route I asked her why she was driving sixty kilometres to Chekina for a swim when she had the beaches of La Crique on her doorstep.

"If you ask a question like that," she replied, "then you can't be much of a beach-goer . . ."

I said that swimming in the sea did indeed fall a long way short of being my greatest passion.

"All the south-side beaches are ghastly, even the one at Cap-Blanc, even the Golf Club beach. They are packed with exhibitionists, body builders, and teenagers trying to fry themselves brown. Maybe I'm a snob, but when I go swimming I like to be left alone, and the more alone I am on a beach, the better I like it . . . "

We got to Chekina about noon. I think it must have been around a hundred degrees. The shore was completely deserted.

The dwellings which line this part of the coast are more like bunkers than villas. They are the virtually inaccessible, internally lavish residences of Grianta's top brass, an aristocracy that despises sand and salt water. The really classy thing in these parts is to have your own slightly refrigerated swimming pool fitted with a wave-making machine. The most sought-after model, the OSS Wavomatic (costing a trifle less than a new Cadillac, before paying for installation), combines "storm and sea-spray simulation" with "programmable wave-height settings from 50 cm to 3 metres," allowing you to perform "On-Station Surfing."

In theory, Chekina beach is not prohibited to anyone. In practice, the only people who ever come here are the few Europeans who have resolved not to take offence if sentries with machine-guns and Rottweilers ogle them through binoculars.

I soon saw why Lise preferred to be on her own on a beach. Scarcely had she set foot on the sand than she untied her pareo with one hand and began to run towards the sea entirely naked.

I'm probably an old fuddy-duddy, but I was at first deeply shocked. I knew that even in countries as backward as Spain and Tunisia it is increasingly the norm, or at any rate tolerated, for women to go swimming with bare breasts or even without any clothes on at all. But my knowledge was exclusively theoretical: I had never had visual confirmation of it; and for a man who must have last had a holiday at the seaside (at La Tranche-sur-Mer) in the mid-1950s, what used to be called "nudists" (or "naturists") were extremely unusual exceptions and the subject of heaps of blue jokes. At Cap-Blanc or La Crique, Lise would have been immediately surrounded, harassed, and perhaps even assaulted by a swarm of repressed adolescents. Here she was the focus only of the lascivious gaze of the guards keeping watch over the houses and the road. No reason why she should give a damn.

I had put on my swimming trunks under my trousers. My one

and only pair of trunks! I had never actually worn them before. I would have liked to take them off. But I didn't dare.

After swimming, we went to lie on a large sisal beachmat in the shade of a tree with fantastically contorted branches and heavy mauve flowers hanging in tight bunches. I didn't dare look at Lise, her beauty overwhelmed me so. My voice was at first somewhat strangulated, but I did manage eventually to tell her of my discovery.

I think it frightened her, as it did me. Even if you're French, you don't usually make light of the BH around here. You talk about it only in roundabout ways; you use figures of speech; it is rare indeed for anyone to say "the BH" openly, you usually refer to "those men," "you know who I mean," "if you catch my drift," and so forth.

We went to have lunch at Les Cigognes. It's a restaurant that is very popular in the evening, but it has little daytime clientèle. For that reason, we were able to have the table next to the giant tortoise pool, and waiters who were much more attentive than usual. Lise seemed lost in thought. Towards the middle of the meal, she said:

"No, however much I rummage around in my mind, I can only see one occasion when Serval mentioned them to me." (More than an hour had passed since I had spoken of the BH, but there was no doubt about the meaning of Lise's "them.")

"What's odd is that it happened on this very spot. That's what has brought it back to mind, otherwise I would probably have forgotten it entirely. Serval had asked me out to dinner. We got here very late, but Dédé agreed to serve us nonetheless – I mean, to serve him; if I had been on my own, he would have sent me packing, I imagine. The restaurant was still bursting at the seams, but nearly everybody else had got to the coffee stage. Soon there was only one other table occupied, but it was quite a company – the whole upper crust of the Embassy was there. Not the Ambassador, but there was the First Secretary, the Trade Attaché, the Technical Counsellor, Saint-Aulaire, Delmont, Mirouet, Levasseur, the whole first eleven. Even your old crony Crozet was there."

"What!" I blurted out in surprise. "You know I know Crozet?"

"But of course I do. I've often seen you two together at Galignani's . . . Anyway, they were drinking champagne . . . I gather they were celebrating Saint-Aulaire's gong. After a while, Dédé made it increasingly clear that his day was done and that he wished to see us clear off.

"We left almost at the same time as the Embassy people. They acknowledged us with nods as we walked past. You probably know that Serval never responded to the pressing advances which the Ambassador made to him almost as soon as he settled here, which so mortified the Ambassador that he virtually gave orders to blackball the writer systematically.

"We had got back into the car and were about to drive off when a shadow approached. It was Mirouet. He asked Serval if he could have a word. Serval thought for a minute, then apologised for leaving me alone for a short while, got out of the car and followed Mirouet. Their conversation lasted a little over half an hour. They talked as they walked up and down the terrace, and I saw Mirouet stop in his tracks several times, and wave his arms about, almost as if he was shouting. But I didn't hear anything of what the two said to each other.

"Serval had an odd look when he got back to the car – he looked facetious and worried at the same time. That's when he spoke to me about the BH.

"'It looks as if that fool has poked his way into a real hornet's nest! And of course he thinks it's a trap set up for him by the Black Hand.'

"'What trap?' I asked.

"'You'll find out soon enough. The muck will be flying around. Anyway, if he really thinks he can get away with it by pinning it all on the Big Bad Wolf, then he's making a great big boo-boo!'

"It was a Friday evening, but it was not until the Monday that I understood what the 'trap' was, when we heard that the statue of Diocletian had been stolen. I suppose you know the story?"

I replied that it had all happened six months before I came to Grianta: "Of course I heard lots of gossip about it! But wasn't it quickly proven that Mirouet had cooked up the whole swindle?"

"The proof was so seamless that people began to insinuate quite openly that the real truth was not quite what was declared to be the official truth . . ."

"And you reckon that *The Crypt* might contain the real truth?"

"I think nothing. I've no opinion. All I said was that it was à propos the Diocletian affair that Serval alluded to the BH in my presence."

We hadn't yet had coffee served when a young militiaman burst into the restaurant where there were now only six customers left including ourselves. He took up position in the centre of the room and politely but firmly invited us to return to Grianta with all due haste before the road was closed.

"I should have guessed," said Lise as she stood up from the table. "It's the same every Thursday. Her Inestimable Ladiness takes tea with some cousin or niece or other, and all the Wazilah grannies assemble to natter, plot, and show off their sparklers to each other. As a consequence no one is allowed to drive on this road from four until eight."

The militiaman's warning had come too late. About twenty kilometres outside Grianta we were halted by chicanes made of black and yellow striped barriers placed across the road. Rather than wait there for four hours beneath the scorching sun we turned on our tracks and then took the side road down to the beach at Cholotcha.

This time I grew bolder, and, like Lise, and in her company, I savoured the pleasure of swimming with no clothes on.

I got home in mid-evening with the image of that young woman whirling around in my mind. Could I possibly be falling in love again? Was I going to lose my head at well past forty-five, and have a fling that would make a cadet blush with shame?

The only relationship of any length that I have had in my time in Grianta has been a mutually unsatisfying affair with Beatrix, which goes on and on petering out. Before, in France, there was everything that I had wanted to leave behind by going into exile abroad. Calm and oblivion were still distant prospects but the old wounds had at least begun to lose their sting. Even if Lise were only a mirage, her bursting in to my life made them less definite, less defined, as if desolation and hope, death and renewal were inextricably intertwined in the same moment. For the first time since the black years after Mathilde's departure I felt that I was emerging from the inexorable absence of desire to which I thought I had been condemned for ever.

I should have called her or rushed round. I should have had the courage. What if she'd laughed in my face? I was afraid of being ridiculous, I was afraid of my age, of my ugliness, of everything about me that was dull, scruffy, flabby, of all those things that made me hate and despise myself.

Towards midnight I was called to the telephone. I lunged for the handset, sure that it must be Lise, as if, by telepathy or by magic, she had been constrained to respond to the seduction-fantasy that I was too cowardly to assume for myself.

A cold and clipped male voice was on the line. My presence was requested. There were things I had to be told. A car would call for me in fifteen minutes. I had no reason to be afraid but should do what I was told.

He hung up. Who was he? Who wanted to say what to me? Who knew about my enquiry, my quasi-detective work? The maddest ideas whizzed through my mind – Serval, the Consul, Lise's lover, the BH, Mirouet. Each possibility set in train a fantasy plot more lunatic than the last and in the end I just gave up guessing.

I waited fourteen minutes, then went down to the street. A limousine was already parked in front of the door – a big black car without number plates. There are plenty such around and they belong to the army, the police, the militia, and the Black Hand; but it was too late to retreat and quite futile to attempt an escape. I could feel the sweat on my hands and my forehead. A man whose face I could not see was standing beside the car, holding the rear door open for me.

I got in. I barely had time to glimpse two dark silhouettes before my head was covered with a hood.

"Relax. There's no danger. As long as you don't know the route we're taking, you're quite safe."

"What you don't know can't hurt you," said another voice on my left.

"Give him a bit more air, you fool, or he'll suffocate," said a third and slightly more distant voice, presumably the voice of the man sitting next to the driver.

They asked me if l wanted to smoke. I said no. They lit up with Virginias.

The journey took a long while, but I would be truly unable to say how long the while lasted, whether it was an age of twenty minutes or of three-quarters of an hour. I know that at one point we were close to the sea, and then went on bumpy roads (but what road is not bumpy, as soon as you leave Grianta city, apart from the tarmac stretches pretentiously called "freeways" which connect the palaces of the President-for-Life?).

The car finally came to a stop in what I thought I could be sure was an underground garage. All four car doors opened almost simultaneously. Hands grabbed my arm, pulled me out, dragged me into an echoing corridor in which our footsteps resounded loudly. I was made to go up four steps. A door opened. I was taken forward a few paces, then forced to sit down in one of those so-called "Saharan" armchairs made of webbing, which you find in plenty in every house in Grianta. I felt my hood being lifted swiftly. Straight after, the door closed on me.

The room in which I found myself was entirely unlit. I stretched my eyes wide open to accustom them to the darkness, to no avail. Then a voice came from a loudspeaker. It was the same voice that had addressed me on the telephone.

"I am sorry to have to ask you to wait a moment. You'll find something to while away the time on the table . . ."

Light burst forth from a ceiling fixture. I saw that I was in a tiny windowless room somewhat like a hospital waiting room. There were benches and chairs around the walls and in the middle was the armchair on which I was sitting, next to a low table laden with a pile of magazines, a cheap glass ashtray, a disposable lighter, a pack of John Bulls (my favourite brand), a stem glass, and a bottle of *grappa* in an ice-bucket. My mysterious interlocutor was obviously well informed about my tastes . . .

I lit a cigarette and poured myself a whole glass of *grappa*. Presumably to calm my nerves I started flicking through the magazine that was on top of the pile. It was an out-of-date issue of

World Cinema. I read almost conscientiously an article about *Raiders of the Lost Ark*, directed by S. Spielberg, an interview with Emmanuèle Riva, and a lengthy biofilmography of Nadine Alari, from which I learned, amongst other things, that her first screen role was in *Jericho*, directed by Henri Calef (1945), that she had played opposite Noël-Noël in *Le Père Tranquille*, opposite Madeleine Robinson in *L'Invité du Mardi*, opposite Martine Carol in *Caroline chérie*, and opposite Simone Renant in *L'Homme de joie*, whilst on stage she had played the fine title role of *Miss Julie*.

The room was abruptly plunged back into darkness. I then heard a long, dull, screeching sound behind me. I turned around: a portion of the wall was sliding back, revealing another room, that was so dimly lit that it took me several seconds to make out the massive outline of a man sitting behind a table. He was probably protected by a thick pane of glass (was that where Serval had got the idea of the interview room in Gotterdam prison???) because his voice came by way of a loudspeaker. But was it his voice? At all events, it was the voice I had already heard twice that evening.

"Good evening, Monsieur Veyraud. Permit me not to introduce myself. It seems you have taken a sufficient interest in me just recently to understand that it would not be in your interest to know my name, my face, or the sound of my voice. We have nothing against you personally and we wish you no harm, please believe that. You have a good job here, a decent salary, and if today is anything to go by, leisure pursuits which would make many of your French compatriots green with envy. So don't play with fire. Don't go sniffing around our patch looking for snakes, which you wouldn't find in any case. If you insist on poking your nose into business that does concern you, then do some more research into your Consul's taste for desert stones. Do you really think he went two or three hundred kilometres into the wastes of Kolorno simply for the pleasure of finding a desert rose or two? Might there not also be a touch of the antiques thief or statue stealer about him?"

Even now, three hours after they brought me back home, I am quite unable to get any sleep and am still struggling to put the pieces of the puzzle back together. What is the Consul suddenly doing in this story? Why, on the very day that Lise mentions Diocletian's statue and Mirouet's recall, does the BH also allude to these things? And how ever does the BH know (unless it has managed to break into this flat and read these very notes) that I "have taken an interest in it just recently"?

CHAPTER ELEVEN

Excavations

Was it all a dream which had vanished in the light of reality? I
looked in the sixth-form history course book and found the
main points of what is known about Grianta in the Roman period and its archaeological remains. From articles in the local
press (diplomatically guarded pieces, but full of sly insinuations),
I pieced together the tremendous scandal of which the only public consequence had been the discreet replacement of Mirouet.
I also got Crozet to reveal a number of things and then I reread
Serval's book in the light of these new clues. I have to concede
that my strange interlocutor was right, that the Black Hand
had nothing to do with the business, but that Serval does in effect
give away a secret in his book, a secret which easily explains why
the *real* culprit may have – no, must have – committed murder.

In the third quarter of the third century, in the reigns of Vale-
rian, Gallienus and Claudius II, most of the generals governing
the provinces of the Roman Empire usurped the purple toga.
They were called the Thirty Tyrants, not because there were thirty
of them – only eighteen are truly known – but in memory of the
Thirty Tyrants of Athens.

In 263, the Governor of Egypt, Emilianus, declared himself
Imperator and took the name of Alexander. But his reign was
short-lived, as were most reigns in that period when soldiers only
seemed to proclaim their leaders emperor the better to slay them
a few months later. Emilianus Alexander was struck down within
a year by one of Gallienus's generals, Theodotus.

Theodotus probably would not have hesitated to crown himself but Gallienus, who had extensive dealings with Sapor, King of Persia, bought the latter's former ally, Odenatus, Prince of Palmyra, and gave him the Empire of the East. Obviously, Odenatus was soon murdered. His widow Zenobia (who in all probability sponsored her husband's assassin) broke away entirely from the control of Rome and for six years, until forced into submission by Aurelian, she held sway over Syria and Egypt.

Meanwhile, one of Emilianus's lieutenants, Marcellus Claudius Burnachus, who had escaped the grasp of Theodotus, regrouped the remnants of the XIth Legion and carved out his own fiefdom in a region which the Romans had never really tackled and which stretched from Thebaidae to Eritrea. It was a vast, fertile area to which traders and settlers soon flocked. Cotton, millet, and sesame grew there in abundance and caravans sallied forth into the mysterious south, returning with cinnamon and myrrh, ivory, gold dust, ostrich feathers, senna, hides, and sometimes caged two-horned rhinoceroses which excited even the most jaded of circus-goers.

On the high plateau of Kolorno, stretching towards the southwestern extremity of the land, lived hostile tribes of Nubians, Nigrites, and Sembrites. To protect his province from their murderous incursions Burnachus set up a fortified camp, which he called Castellum Acridium, at the foot of the mountain pass that provided the route from the plateau to the central lowlands.

Protected by his very remoteness, Burnachus remained in power without too much trouble even after Probus, Carus and Numerianus had reasserted imperial authority and unseated one by one those of the usurpers who had not done for each other already. But things began to change when Diocletian reigned. With the establishment of the Tetrarchy, the grip of central authority over the furthest reaches of the empire began to tighten. The disturbances which broke out in Tripolitania and Cyrenaica in the 290s brought the intervention of Maximianus himself, and Burnachus, who was not at all eager to launch a campaign he was very likely to lose, surrendered of his own free will. He put it to Maximianus that he had succeeded in preserving the outer bounds of the Roman *limes*, and that under his aegis, Castellum Acridium and Gradus Antiqui had become flourishing cities that could rival Hippo, Lepcis or Hadrumetae.

Since Maximianus had other pisces to fritare, particularly in Mauretania and in Egypt, he was happy to make a pact with Burnachus, whom he made king of *Aethiopia supra Aegyptum*, and for whom he reinvented the old honorific title of "Friend of the Roman People," *amicus populi romani*. It was to give concrete form to this alliance that Burnachus had a huge nymphaeum or shrine built at Castellum Acridium, its main fountain adorned with four colossal statues of the Emperors of the Tetrarchy: Diocletian and Maximianus, the two Augustuses, Constantius Chlorus and Galerius, and the two Caesars. But it didn't stop Burnachus from getting himself slain a few months later.*

In the course of the following centuries, the Persians, the Vandals, the Funji negroes, and the Arabs took and retook the region in turn. The only true victor was the desert sand. By the end of the eighteenth century Grianta was the capital and virtually the sole inhabited township of a narrow coastal emirate where desert caravans and Mediterranean seafarers met to barter. Then a few decades later the Western powers began to take an interest in such apparently barren places with a subsoil rich in phosphates, potassium, manganese, cobalt, and much else.

The first archaeological surveys were done in the 1860s by the Italians Manzi and Bucci. They were not concerned with Roman ruins but with an attempt to locate (and possibly to find traces of) the *Kaabat-al-Maa* (its full name is *Kaabat-Min-Kabl-al Bahr*, i.e. "the Kaaba before (this side of) the sea," but it has always been referred to as *Kaabat-al-Maa*, "the water Kaaba," in distinction to "the desert Kaaba" at Mecca). As is well known, the Kaaba is the more or less cubic edifice in the centre of the Great Mosque at

---

*It is said that Maximianus entrusted him with a secret message to deliver to Diocletian, then residing at Nicomedæ. Diocletian received the message, opened the seal and read: "He who brings this is to be put to death without delay." The instruction was executed, and Burnachus by the same token.

The anecdote, reported by Ammianus Marcellinus, seems too much of a conscious imitation of Suetonius (who attributes the device to Caligula) to be accepted without reservation. Moreover, it is found in various forms in dozens of authors, who relate it to Marius and Bocchus, to Theodoric and Merovius, to the Guelfs and the Ghibellines and to the Farneses and the Sforzas.

Mecca, in the northeastern corner of which is set the famous Black Stone which all *hadji* pilgrims come to kiss. For Muslims, the Kaaba is the centre of the world, and it is towards the Kaaba that they turn when they prostrate themselves to pray.

In the fourth and fifth centuries of the Hegira, Grianta came under the sway of a schismatic sect, the Hunaites (from *huna*, "here"). The Hunaites claimed that Allah was everywhere and that it was not only pointless but impious to travel in order to honour him. They therefore constructed a faithful replica of the Meccan Kaaba in the courtyard of the Grianta mosque, which they capped in like manner with a *kiswa* (a covering of black brocade), provided with a single entrance accessible by means of a removable step-ladder, and they cemented into its eastern corner a black stone.

The Hunaites were modest heretics. They did not seek to start a holy war to spread their faith. In one of his Maquâmât, Hariri mocks them rather benignly, saying through Abu Zayd that they are as good Muslims as any other, but that their faith has no sea legs.* Very few theologians really tore into them but the Hunaites nonetheless came to a sorry end. As vassals of the Cairene Fatimids, who tolerated their heresy, they were exterminated when Salâh-al-Din (Saladin) imposed 'Abâssid sovereignty and observance of the *sunna* ("tradition") over Egypt. The sacrilegious *kaaba* was razed to the ground. In its place, a caravanserai was put up as a resting stage for pilgrims en route to the Holy City.

Part of the caravanserai was still standing in the nineteenth century, and Manzi and Bucci hoped to find beneath its foundations the remains of the *Kaabat-al-Maa* and perhaps even the Black Stone itself. But their search was fruitless.

At the start of French colonisation, soldiers and missionaries with a passion for archaeology began excavating Gradus Antiqui, the remains of which stand a few kilometres northwest of present-day Grianta. It soon became apparent that Gradus Antiqui was one of the best preserved cities of Roman Africa, and though it was considerably later than Ptolemais or Cyrene it was infinitely richer than they were from an architectural, urban, and artistic point of view. Even today there is more than a third of the city still undug,

---

*The pun cannot be rendered into French.

and not a year goes by without priceless pieces being unearthed, as a consequence of which the museum of antiquities at Grianta, though small in size, is one of the foremost of its kind in the world.

For a long period, Gradus Antiqui was thought to be the southernmost of all the cities that the Romans built. It was only in 1942 that Warmington expressed the view, which he based on a controversial reading of fragments of Eutropius and Paulus Orosius, that in order to protect their city the Romans must have established an oppidum far to the south, in the proximity of the high plateaux where there lived tribes known to be markedly hostile to Roman civilisation. This hypothesis was widely attacked by specialists, most of whom considered the role of Gradus Antiqui to have been exclusively of a maritime nature, the hinterland having never been sufficiently developed to attract the destructive greed of tribes living more than eighty kilometres away. But some years later an aerial survey of the country carried out by the French National Geographical Institute in preparation of a 1:80,000 scale map showed clearly that there was a *decumanus maximus* at the foot of Sakka Pass, proving beyond dispute that a permanent military encampment really had existed more than one hundred kilometres south of Grianta.

The turmoil that preceded independence delayed the start of excavations. However, a small French archaeological expedition had the good fortune to discover an inscription which, in Pflaum's reading, was to allow the whole history of Castellum Acridium and Gradus Antiqui to be put back together and to take the form in which we know it today. The inscription is reconstituted as follows:

PRO SALUTE IMP[ERATORIS]
M[ARCI] AURELI VALERII MAXIMIANI
HERCULII
OB ÆTHIOPES ET NUBIOS VICTOS
. . . . . .
MARCELLUS CLAUD[IUS] BURN . . .
REX AMI[CUS] P[OPULI] R[OMANI]
. . .

The excavations began in earnest at Castellum Acridium in 1979, a year before my arrival. They were conducted by a team of American researchers from Fitchwinder University at Swetham (MA), under the direction of Professor Shetland. Thanks to super-sophisticated tools, notably a laser probe, used here for the first time, the archaeologists took but a few weeks to raise the fabulous if somewhat sand-eaten remains of a major Roman encampment. The discovery of the nymphaeum was both bedazzling and disappointing, for although the grandiose design of the ensemble was perfectly obvious, almost all of its constituent parts were pretty well irrecoverable. Of the four colossal statues of the Emperors, only one – of Diocletian – had by some miracle remained intact.

The endless negotiations which had preceded the start of the dig were concerned in particular with the apportionment of the "works of art and other valuable remains" between the three institutions cosponsoring the project: the Office of Culture (responsible for the Grianta Museum of Archaeology), the French Foreign Ministry (representing CENA, the Centre for Ancient Epigraphy and Numismatics at Sophia-Antipolis), and UNESCO, which was responsible for managing the American grants awarded to Professor Shetland. One hundred and seventy-one meetings, each more exhausting than the other, were needed to decide what would happen to each category of find – coins and medals, jewels, weapons, earthenware, ceramics, funerary urns, and so on – which would go, in one case or another, to this or that specialised institute or be deposited with the Grianta State Museum until a site museum was built at Castellum Acridium or would bolster the holdings of the so-called National Heritage Office, the most likely location of which was one of the President-for-Life's Swiss bank safes.

Monumental statues, if there were any, would be the legal property of UNESCO, which accepted the costs of exhibiting them for longer or shorter periods (from two to six years) in the world's main museums of antiquities (Naples, the Thermae in Rome, the Louvre, Athens, Cairo, the Smithsonian, Munich, Istanbul, Syracuse, the University of Philadelphia, etc.), the choice of museums to be made by lottery.

The luck of the draw most conveniently attributed the statue of Diocletian to the Louvre, which allowed its first showing to coincide exactly with the President-for-Life's official visit to France, scheduled for mid-March 1980.

The technical details of the operation were entrusted to the French Cultural Institute of Grianta, which had the Diocletian stored in a dockside warehouse and commissioned the construction of the supporting frame which would be needed to lift the statue into a shipping container.

Unfortunately, when the staff of the Louvre opened the crate on 3 March 1980 they discovered that it contained only a consignment of glazed earthenware destined for the Burchell Foundation.

One might well have feared at that point that the strengthening of the traditional links between Grianta and Paris would be deferred *sine die*. However, at the last minute a chryselephantine Juno was discovered at Gradus Antiqui, and though it was tiny next to the Diocletian (and despite the fact that the Louvre already had at least half a dozen), it suited everyone's purpose, except perhaps for the head of the President-for-Life's private secretariat who had to rewrite the inauguration speech from start to finish, replacing all the references to Rome and its Empire with allusions to Juno Coelestis, a no less inexhaustible topic, to be sure, but one far less amenable to the historico-political purple prose which was supposed to allow the President-for-Life to stride down the centuries to the matters that were closest to his heart – increased military aid and the renewal of technical assistance contracts.

The Louvre had earthenware instead of Diocletian, but the Burchell Foundation did not get Diocletian instead of earthenware. The statue had not just been mislaid, it had been abducted. It was soon learned from Professor Shetland (who gave few details) that even before the dig began an American billionaire had, so to speak, "ordered" a statue of a Roman deity or Emperor to decorate the monumental staircase in his front hall. Obviously his name was not divulged, but he had given Shetland to understand that he was minded to go as high as one million dollars if his order could be met. "Has to be a statue that's worth it, of course," said the middleman who had contacted Shetland. "Don't gimme a garden gnome, OK? Something real fancy, like a Winged Victory of Trasimene or a Venus de Milo, OK?"

Shetland declined the offer which hardly fitted his vocation, and as soon as he got to Grianta he warned the local authorities that attempts at bribery and corruption were likely to take place on the site. As a result the dig began with a small armed guard making sure (or pretending to make sure) that the workmen didn't damage the jewels and medals which they came upon with their picks. In fact, the workmen, the soldiers and the site foremen were entirely well disposed to being got round, and did deals on everything they knew to be dealable, but there's a hell of long way from that to making off with a statue weighing several tons!

The enquiry into the theft failed to clarify even the most basic point, whether the statue had gone missing on the site, in transit to Grianta, from the docks, from the container ship which took it to Marseille, or en route from Marseille to the Department of Classical Antiquities at the Louvre.

The only thing which could be taken as fairly sure was that the American collector had not backed off after his rebuff but had done a deal with someone else. That someone else must have been very highly placed indeed.

Searches of the offices of French officials brought to light an extremely compromising document in the possession of Mirouet. It was the file copy of a letter dated 26 December 1979 to a certain Fabian D. Donaldson, "Curator of the AAA" (American Association of Antiquarians), describing the statue of Diocletian in very precise detail. Mirouet made no bones about that letter: Donaldson had written to him, he said, in connection with the survey article he was doing of that year's excavations of Roman antiquities for the *Annual Review of Archaeological Research*. It was easily established that the scholarly journal existed, that it did publish annual surveys of current research in Sumerian, Aramaic, Hebrew, Minoan, Greek, Etruscan, Egyptian, Celtic and other fields of archaeological exploration, and that no one called Donaldson had had anything to do with that year's report on the Roman period.

But there was worse to come. When Mirouet's movements

between October 1979 and March 1980 were reconstituted, it transpired that he had travelled to Europe on two occasions. To Paris, the diplomat claimed – with stopovers in Zürich and Geneva, the investigators riposted. According to a confidential brief from the Revenue Inspectors, Mirouet had opened two accounts, at the Geneva Credit Bank and the Appenzell Banking Company, in which he deposited US $125,271 and US $241,200 respectively. Mirouet vehemently denied both the stopovers and the deposits. He had gone to France for perfectly regular reasons, he protested; on the first occasion, as the examiner of a doctoral dissertation on Louise Labbé (a writer on whom he was an authority), and on the second occasion for the midwinter school holidays.

But the accusations against him were too grave, and on 7 March 1980 he was recalled to Paris.

In fact, he never appeared before the committee of enquiry set up to consider his case. There was a trial; Mirouet was convicted *in absentia*; and his contempt of court gave credibility to the official presumption of his guilt. But that did not stop most people from insinuating (in Grianta, the contrary would have been amazing) that Mirouet was no more than the man who had been made to carry the can.

CHAPTER TWELVE

Frightening thoughts

Crozet has let me see several police reports. From one of them I've learned the names of two of the intermediaries in the affair of the American art collector and the supplier of Diocletian. One is called Bulow and usually lives in Lisbon; he's an operator who has been involved in many shady, not to say illegal, affairs. The other is a London antiquarian called Joseph Boss, whose speciality is gold-topped walking-sticks. (In *The Magistrate is the Murderer*, the sting is built around Fly being a collector of walking-sticks. Coincidence?)

Another one of the police reports deals at length with the fall of the Griantese Ministry of Culture. The minister, known to all and sundry as Granpa, is the President-for-Life's uncle, and he is alleged to have had the devil's own trouble in persuading his nephew that he had nothing to do with the Diocletian business. The President-for-Life was hopping mad because several high-ranking French officials had hinted that gestures of that kind might have helped to raise his name for a Nobel Peace Prize.

The French Ambassador had almost been busted, but the Foreign Ministry thought it desirable not to make matters worse, and the recall of Mirouet was the only action which the government took over the whole episode.

I thought that all these new puzzle pieces would make it easier to figure out the truth that Serval had put in *The Crypt*. In fact he only makes a brief allusion to the statue on page 32, and none of his hints points significantly towards a supposedly "real" culprit.

In *The Crypt*, the theft of the statue of Diocletian is transformed into the business of negotiating the sale of the Arethusa MTBs. The deal between the French and Fernland is upset by an American, in the same way that Grianta's gift of a statue to Paris is upset by an American. Arethusa was a nymph turned into a spring, a transparent reference to the classical nymphaeum and its fountain. The names of the four emperors of the Tetrarchy whose statues adorned the said fountain are combined as an acronym in a very secondary character, the Argentinian architect who dances with Anne Svendsen: Di Magalco.

> DI ocletian
> MA ximianus
> GAL erius
> CO nstantius Chlorus

As for the Arethusa's weaponry, it refers back to Burnachus:

> MCB 1000 S = Marcellus Claudius Burnachus Miles
> RAPR   = Rex Amicus Populi Romani

The typescript ends here.

CHAPTER TWELVE
(continued)

I shall recapitulate briefly. An American megalomaniac has engaged in murky machinations to lay his hands on a statue of Diocletian unearthed at the site of Castellum Acridium, near Sakka Pass, in the region of Kolorno, in Grianta.

The French cultural attaché, Mirouet, is taken to be the American's accomplice. He is recalled to Paris, where he goes to ground, but before disappearing he speaks at length to Robert Serval. According to what Serval told Lise about that conversation, Mirouet claimed to be the fall guy of a scam set up by the Black Hand. Serval investigates, discovers the truth and tells it in his own way in a book called *The Crypt*. Fearing for his life, he gives the typescript to the Consul who then asks me to examine it.

Meanwhile, the Black Hand hauls me in, asserts that it had nothing to do with the affair, and hints that the Consul may well be mixed up in it.

Ring-file 2

Mirouet had been manipulated from start to finish not by the BH (as he must also have told Serval), but by the Consul (and so my mysterious interlocutor had not been lying).

In the process of cross-checking, Serval found proof of the Consul's guilt. And that is where the Machiavellian cunning of the whole thing comes into daylight at last: Serval encrypts this manifestly dangerous truth in an *unfinished* detective story which he gets the Consul himself to read.

The Consul quickly grasps that he is being black-mailed directly: unless he complies, the book's ending will be so cast as to put the only too obvious culprit, Rouard-Mirouet, in the clear.

Ring-file 6

At first glance you can't see what connection there is between the theft of a statue weighing several tons and desert outings.

Nonetheless, it is obvious that the Consul is one of the few people in a sufficiently powerful position to think up, carry out, and get away with a crime of that kind.

But in that case why the devil should Serval, when he discovers the truth, have it read specifically by the culprit himself?

It's absolute madness!

Or is it the high point of his cunning, or, more exactly, a blackmail operation?

What I mean is: Serval has the Consul read his book. That says: if this book comes out, then everyone, dear Consul, will know that you stole the statue.

So: pay up: half and half: $500,000.

Ring-file 3

Frightening thoughts
The Diocletian affair has left only tiny traces in *The Crypt* and they are practically impossible to interpret:
    – Arethusa = a nymph turned into a spring = nymphaeum and fountain.

– DiMagalco = acronym of the tetrarchy.
– MCB 1000 S =
– RAPR =
You could add ROUARD = MIROUET, especially if you take R's first name into account (given once only)

REMIROU ARD
AND REMIROU ET

And that's all. Not enough to pin guilt on anyone.
I went to bed early. Couldn't get to sleep. Around ten p.m. the transparent, awful truth came to me:

Mirouet was manipulated, not by the BH as he says to Serval, but by the Consul (as the BH told me). Serval has proof of the Consul's guilt. He allows the latter to know it, by showing him his book *without an ending*: the dénouement would show the Consul's guilt.

Why? Because he has big financial problems (gambling debts).

Ring-file 1

None of these elements allows me to go any further or to try to imagine who else could have pulled it off. On reflection practically everybody could have done it, I mean, any petty port official at Grianta, or a customs officer, or the director of the harbour police, or a couple of crane drivers in cahoots with the container ship's lading officer (because of the heat, ships are loaded at night). Not to mention the few days when the statue was in a warehouse at the dockside at Grianta. There was nothing to prevent the Ambassador, for instance, from having the artic (the embassy truck-trailer) making a detour on its way from Castellum Acridium to Grianta. Etc., etc., etc.

So between 17 December 1979, when it was

unearthed, and 3 March 1980, when the deception was discovered, three score and more different people were in a position to get hold of it (the statue of Diocletian). It would certainly have been easier to do that than to pin the theft on Mirouet.

I am horribly disappointed. I expected Serval's book to give me a clear sign, something that lifted the veil clearly and unambiguously on the *real* culprit, on the man who when he knew he was uncovered had no option but murder!

I don't know what the time was when I woke up in a start. The bed was soaked in sweat: the truth, the luminous and fearful, transparent and awful truth had just struck me.

Ring-file 12

Then the luminous and fearful truth came to me: the Consul had understood that Serval was blackmailing him, and had responded in the most efficient way – by killing him.

Then he cooked up his comedy so that by a means I had not yet fathomed the culprit would end up being me!

Ring-file 5

Frightening thoughts
A set-up by Serval in order to blackmail the Consul
OR
a comedy scripted by the Consul so as to murder Serval and steal his manuscript, which proves that the Consul did it.

He destroys the ending, the "real proof"
so Lise would have to be an accomplice!

Ring-file 16

The Consul pretends (for my benefit) not to understand the text at all.

In fact he sees right through it and he *kills Serval*.

Why did he give me the job of investigating the book? Because he'll use my investigation *to pin Serval's murder on me*.

Blue 31

The Narrator is more and more in love with Lise.

At the same time the "frightening thought" forms in his mind – that the Consul killed Serval and is in the process of pinning the crime on him.

It's an intuition. The book contains no hidden truth, it was just a decoy, a pretext.

no real clue   or else the revolver?

Lise telephones him in a panic, he dashes round in a taxi, rings the bell. The door is open. He hears a shot, rushes up to the bedroom and discovers the Consul's corpse!

Ring-file 33

The narrator finds a corpse but it is the Consul's, not Serval's. Serval killed the Consul: in carrying out his investigation, the Narrator has merely set up the trail which will incriminate him (motive, the weapon of the crime, the opportunity, the witness, etc.).

CHAPTER THIRTEEN

Blue 32

The police came to arrest me next day at five a.m.

I was expecting it and had not tried to flee.

I don't know how they managed it but I know that I have no chance. "They," I suppose, are Lise and Serval, who faked his own disappearance and planned the crime which I would inexorably appear to have committed.

I'm sure my fingerprints are on the revolver and that someone saw me come out looking dazed, in a total panic.

All night long I have been thinking over the affair. Why choose me, etc. . . .

Reconstitution of the affair, just as the book (*The Crypt*) led the narrator's investigation.

Obviously I'll show this diary to the Grianta police, but I'm not under any illusions.

Ring-file 37

I don't know when they decided on a poor provincial teacher as their fall guy. Probably after the Consul gave me the job of running the French book stand.

They knew the Consul was going to go to France and that it would be easy for Serval to ask him to give me the manuscript.

At first I thought that the events which shook Grianta six weeks ago had got in the way of their plans. But what with the repeated taunts from the entourage of the Interior Minister, it wasn't hard to predict that the twenty-fifth anniversary of independence would trigger off riots and bloodshed. On the contrary, it helped them a lot . . .

How did they manage to ensure that I would meet Lise and unwittingly follow the trails, or rather the traps, that she had set for me? What if I had never thought of going to look for that fake typist? I suppose they would have coped in some other way, but they must have been sure that I would be hooked by that missing chapter.

Blue 30

The four clues which will do for the narrator:
A   he will be in Lise's company (motive)
B   his prints will be on the gun
C   a witness sees him go into the Consul's at the time of the murder and come out looking crazy
D

Ring-file 34

I suppose that even the choice of typewriter was dictated by the fact that I knew the supplier well.

Ring-file 35

There is no safer place for a fly to land on than the fly-trap he might otherwise fly into

Lichtenberg

Ring-file 38

Yes of course I'll give this diary to the examining

magistrate. But how could I cherish the illusion that it will help me.

How can those infinitely malleable things called words ever prove anything other than the useless subtlety of rhetoric?

II

"Un R est un M qui se
P le L de la R"

Epigraph: Snow as a proof sheet

CHAPTER FOURTEEN

[Robert Serval, a businessman and former member of the French Resistance, has disappeared. In his car, found abandoned near Grenoble, there is a manuscript. It is called 53 Days]

Ring-file 39

Robert Serval's disappearance

Items of the investigation:
    car
    revolver
    attaché case
    53 Days identification of typewriter? and of typing

Life of Robert Serval.

MARKING TIME

53 Days studied by a critic

Eventually, Salini is called in

Ring-file 40

Meanwhile, Madame Serval, etc.

Salini looks things over

It is a middle-class drawing room, etc.

The disappearance of Robert Serval made a splash in the papers:

> Robert Serval, who was decorated for his work in the Resistance and went on to serve as a member of parliament and then as a minister of state, was, as he approached the age of sixty, an exemplary businessman whose energy and dynamism have contributed to making France what she is today.

At any rate, that's what a mass-circulation weekly said.

Ring-file 42

Robert Serval, alias Louviers

Born Rouen, 1918
Education
Hobbies
Travels
Holidays

Joins the Resistance in ?
first at Grenoble, where he runs a bookshop which serves as a dead-letter box. The letter box is discovered and he flees to the mountains of the Chartreuse.

Becomes a leader of the maquis (FFI) in 43 (?) in the Grande Chartreuse (after the death of his superior, Captain X, a professional soldier).

The British commando affair?

Involved in street fighting when Grenoble is liberated.
Volunteers: Colmar, etc.
Croix de guerre, médaille de la Résistance, médaille militaire, etc.

Demobbed in 45
Finishes degree in business law?
Goes into politics around '48. Mayor of ? Regional councillor
MP in 59
Widower in '64 (aged 46), remarries a 25-year-old American in '66
Secretary of State for Foreign Trade in 1972
His time at the ministry turns out to be profitable for the businesses he deals with
No scandal, but suspicions
Retires from politics in '74
Businesses: textile mills, clothes manufacturing, vegetable fibres (coconut, raffia, matting fibres, etc.)
Frequent travels to Africa, Middle East, Far East, America
Divorce pending in 1981. Separated from his wife Patricia née Humphrey (b. 1941).

Ring-file 41

The facts of the case
The investigation makes no headway
The investigation makes no headway
Our only hope, Salini is told, is for that mysterious manuscript to contain, in one form or another, the key to our problem.
At the moment we still don't know whether Serval is dead or alive.
If he is dead, where is the body?
Everything leads us to believe that the document has something to do with Serval's disappearance.
We had it read by a publisher. He said it was pretty superficial as a "mystery" but quite full of puzzling details nonetheless.
You'll find all that in the files.

CHAPTER FIFTEEN

Ring-file 43

Salini:

The so-called Serval finds the solution to the Rouard affair in a book.

The unfortunate narrator of *53 Days* is supposed to find the key to the puzzle of Serval's faked disappearance in a book.

So Salini also sought the cause of Serval's quite genuine death in a book.

Bedside 2

Salini reads *53 Days*, rereads it once, twice 3 times 4 times.

He doesn't know what to do with Madame Serval. He lists the allusions to Serval in *53 Days*.

Ring-file 44

The author of *53 Days* lays many false trails. For instance, Robert Serval is the model not only for the character of Robert Serval, but for the Consul and the narrator too. Like the Consul, Serval was born at Rouen without being of Norman ascent; like the narrator, he had spent several holidays at Veulle-les-Roses. There were too many details of this kind for them all to be coincidental. Even very minor characters with no direct relevance to the detective plot had been given some of Robert Serval's traits – for instance, the club tie with which Grace Hillof was strangled was his (nothing to do with the entirely fictional Blackbells Military Academy of Arizona: the purely decorative crest was

that of the Florida Spinners' Guild, which had made
Serval "Honorary Spindle" during the French–American Trade Week at Miami, thought up and promoted
by Serval).

CHAPTER SIXTEEN

Bedside 2

Grianta? Etampes? Names of people, places, etc.?

Ring-file 45

In *53 Days* how does Salini interpret Etampes? Does he
investigate or does he decide that Etampes = Bordeaux
(for instance) where Serval did his degree?
HE MUST make something of it (make it mean
something quite different)

CHAPTER SEVENTEEN

Ring-file 46

So it is in *53 Days* and nothing else that Salini has a
chance of finding something that will get the case off
the ground.

Rhodia 13

In between the last two pages of the typescript is a strip
of paper bearing this mysterious formula
"Un R est un M qui se P le L de la R"

Ring-file 47

"Un R est un M qui se P le L de la R." He keeps coming back to this cryptic code. He's tried working it out,
pages and pages of workings-out. He gives the problem
to everyone he bumps into.

> [*The solution is*: Un Roman est un Miroir qui se
> Promène le Long de la Route, "*a novel is a mirror
> walking along a road,*" a version of Stendhal's cele-
> brated definition of the novel]

CHAPTER EIGHTEEN

Ring-file 64

As for the allusions which led to Stendhal, there were so
many that Salini gave up listing them all. In *53 Days*,
Robert Serval had a *red* Jaguar, in life he had a *black*
one. At the Hilton, the Consul chose to eat a veal cutlet
with spinach as if by chance, but it was of course Stendhal's favourite dish. Cularo is the name of the village
which became Grenoble [Stendhal's birthplace] centuries later; Grianta is the name of the castle on the shore

of Lake Como where Fabrice del Dongo [the hero of *La Chartreuse de Parme*] spent his childhood, etc.

In *The Magistrate is the Murderer*, Angèle (Angelina) is found dead in her flat in Rue Saint-Séverin (San severina), whilst the four deaths in *The Koala Case Mystery** occur in a house in Nasturtium Street, a translation of "Rue des Capucines," where Stendhal was struck down by apoplexy. One of Stendhal's addresses, 8 Rue de Caumartin (where he wrote *La Chartreuse de Parme*, in fact), is given as that of the narrator of *53 Days* during his student years in Paris; as for Serval's real address, 71 Rue Murillo, in the Parc Monceau district, it appears in *The Crypt* curiously transmogrified into 71 Calle del Moreau, in Muncillo.

Bedside 2

The frequency of the word mirror and its cognates.

Ring-file 65

Salini reads *53 Days*, and ends up finding Stendhal. But what Stendhal? The epigraph: snow, Saint-Réal: Chambéry.
Speculation on reality and mirrors.
Allusions to *La Chartreuse*.
THEREFORE led back to the Chartreuse maquis.

---

* Given in English in the original, as are many other words and phrases.

Other 10

Clues from *La Chartreuse de Parme*
(or from *The Red and the Black*)

What's at stake is making Salini find out that the affair took place between Grenoble and Chambéry (somewhere along that road), in the Chartreuse massif. therefore clues which make reference to names

The only thing that's clear from the start is that the novels have *nothing* in common with each other apart from the fact that Serval is *also* the name of a central character in *53 Days*.

Even if Serval had the book in front of him it would mean *nothing*. He has nothing to do with a hot country or a cold one, has never murdered a consul.

CHAPTER NINETEEN (& TWENTY, & TWENTY-ONE)

Ring-file 76

The whole career of Serval, alias Louviers, in the Resistance is reconstituted (the pseudonym is not the hero).

Joins Resistance
Dead-letter box
Forged papers
Avoids STO *[Compulsory Labour Service in Germany]*
Helps the British
The Chartreuse

The COMMANDO

The affair of the cave at . . .
his sorties
the survivors

– The Hardy affair?
– insurmountable difficulties of reconstruction

Ring-file 77

Serval's code-name was Louviers.

At a banquet held by former members of the Resistance, which Serval had been asked to chair when he was still undersecretary of state, he explained how he had chosen his pseudonym. He thought first of Rouen, because that was where he was born. But his CO explained that he would be taking an unnecessary risk. The Gestapo and the Paramilitary Police employed specialists to decode pseudonyms. Some of them were really quite bright. One was even said to have found the real name of one of the leaders of the maquis in the Creuse from two *noms de guerre* which he had used in succession, having been obliged to drop the first

Ring-file 78

after his liaison agents had been caught. First he was called *Persée* ("Perseus"), and then *Fleury* ("Flowery").
    What is the real name of a chap who takes the name *Persée* and then *Fleury*?
    The specialist got it in one: *Panier,** and he was right: the guy really was called Pannier.

---

*Panier percé and *panier fleuri* are two fixed expressions in French. Very roughly, it's as if an Englishman called *Baskett* had taken "Whicker" and then "Ball" as his *noms de guerre*.

In fact, Salini notes, Louviers is but the consonantal palindrome of SERVAL
SRVL – LouVieRS

Ring-file 79

List of the commando dropped into the Chartreuse (Operation " ")
hidden by Serval in the . . . cave in the Chartreuse, then, in the cave, all arrested.
An internal landing was planned (Vercors, Massif Central, Chartreuse) and this drop was an advance party.

Ring-file 83

The British commando (OSS?) consisted of 5 Englishmen, Sutherland, Oatley, Mortdale, Penshurt, Sydenham; 3 Canadians, Redfern, Rockdale, Hurstville; 1 New Zealander, Kogarah; 2 Frenchmen, Tempe, Como; 1 Lebanese, Jannali. Hidden in a building at the Chartreuse monastery for 48 hours then taken to a cave.
And then?
The militiamen surrounding the cave slaughtered everyone except the commando's CO and Serval alias Bérot, who were handed over to the Gestapo.
Post-war investigation.
Who betrayed them? (if they were betrayed)
Bérot, who escaped and was later decorated?
Sutherland?
PROBLEM; the instigators of *53 Days* must be French.
Let's say Tempe and Como are French (Free French).
Forét des Meuniers *[?]* Gorges de Malessard.

Ring-file 81

What Serval Louviers really did in the Resistance.
A – runs bookshop-letter box
B – flees to the Chartreuse
C – takes the British commando to the cave
Two days later, the commando is handed over to another group of the maquis, and they are ambushed. All killed on the spot except Sébastien Tempe (a Frenchman in the SOE) and   alias Chabert, the leader of the other group. After interrogation and torture, Tempe is imprisoned at   , whence he manages to escape.   alias Chabert vanishes.
After the war, there is an enquiry based on Tempe's account. Louviers's name is mentioned, favourably for the most part. A search is made for Chabert. But in vain. (Let's suppose Chabert is dead.)

D – takes part in the fighting to liberate Grenoble
E – goes to fight in Alsace.
AND THAT'S ALL
Patricia: There was nothing heroic about Serval, nor was he remotely like a traitor. Wouldn't have known how. Swept along by events.

When "the Consul" and Patricia decide on their coup, they agree that "the Consul" will play the role of a "Chabert" who has proof of Louviers's guilt, finds Tempe, and murders Louviers. So far so good. But what does Tempe say?

Other 11

What do you know when you've read the novel to the end? Nothing, except that for quite unknown reasons Serval has been given the manuscript of a detective story one of whose protagonists (the one you think is the victim until he is finally unmasked as the culprit) has the same name as he does. You can see straight away that this single clue has a deeper meaning: that Serval, who is believed to be innocent, is in fact guilty, and that the person or persons who murdered him did so by means and for reasons which are given somewhere in the book. The truth is in the book, is encrypted in it, in exactly the same way that the investigation which culminates in the incrimination of the unwitting narrator of *53 Days* is conducted on the basis of clues provided by the manuscript entitled *The Crypt*.

But when you can see that, you see nothing; the affair might be to do with a woman, or connected with Madame Serval, or with a mistress of Serval's, or it might be related to Serval's business interests, or to his political affairs, or to the part he played in the Resistance.

not a thing

Ring-file 88

Or else the man who calls himself R. Serval and passes for a former hero of the Resistance, code-name Bérot, alias Louviers, is in reality Barbinet, head of the ? militia (who arrested, tortured, and killed RS and took his place on xx 1944).

Or else he *went over* after arrest by the Gestapo and is in fact responsible for the capture of the entire maquis group.

In case 1: 2 former maquis of RS's group recognise him

In case 2: 2 survivors of RS's group (the "Consul" and X) obtain proof of his treachery and execute him.

Ring-file 85

This is what Salini said to Inspector H:
It is now clear to me that the disappearance and
in all probability the murder of Serval are connected
with what happened a few weeks before the liberation
of Grenoble (Sept. 44?) in the mountains of La Grande
Chartreuse, between Grenoble and Chambéry. That is
what the book clearly hints at and it offers no other
lead.
The Intelligence Service file on Serval is not a thick
one. It shows that Serval joined the Resistance in Lyon
in 1942; one of his old school chums was part of an
intelligence network which looked after airmen who
had baled out over France, and helped to get them back
to Britain. He asked Serval to run a little bookshop
used by the network as a letter box. A few weeks later
the letter box was blown.

Ring-file 82

I propose to take you to that cave in the forest of
to find the corpse of Robert Serval.

CHAPTER TWENTY-TWO

Ring-file 90

Salini deciphers the enigma of "Un R est un M qui se
P le L de la R," and draws from it these conclusions: if
there is a hidden message in the book, then it is probably something like "things are not what they seem (or

seemed) to be." In *The Crypt*, the detective-narrator Serval investigates the death of Rouard to discover that the murderer is Vichard, but the aforementioned Rouard is not dead at all; his faked death is the tool of a perfect crime whose victim would have been Vichard if Serval had not uncovered the "real truth." In *53 Days*, the anonymous narrator believes the Consul has killed Serval, and is trying to get him to carry the can; whereas the truth is the opposite – Serval, with the assistance of Lise, has killed the Consul and has set things up so that the narrator-detective is inexorably incriminated. "Reality" is thus the opposite of what you first think, and the problem is to choose one of the many possible opposites. It's quite possible that Serval isn't dead; it's quite possible that he is dead, but that the murderer is not X as we are led to believe, but Y; it's quite possible that Serval has taken his own life and wants to pin his death on X, or on Y . . .

The narrator of *53 Days* says, à propos of *The Crypt*: "In Serval's novels, as with Ellery Queen and others, the author's pseudonym is the same as the name of his hero." If we take this sentence as a clue to Serval's disappearance, how should we read it? In the novels of Ellery Queen, and this can be checked easily, the hero's name and the authors' *nom-de-plume* are indeed identical. In his "real" life, Serval-*nom-de-guerre*, that is to say Serval alias Bérot in the Resistance, was also a Hero. Is that what is wrong? Is that what the unknown author of *53 Days* is trying to tell us? – That the *nom-de-plume* is NOT the hero; Serval alias Bérot is NOT a hero: HE IS A TRAITOR.

There is something nightmarish about all of this. Salini finds himself in the same position as the narrator of *53 Days*, and at times the namelessness of that narrator plunges him into a curious state of anxiety, to the point where he almost wonders if he hasn't been explicitly designated by the author to conduct this most unusual investigation. The idea is patently absurd. Before being asked to take the case on, he knew neither Serval nor his wife, but he can't help identifying with the amateur detective who is so easily led astray. Sometimes he feels the need to reassure himself by going through all the features which distinguish him from the narrator-character – he's twenty years older, he's never been a French teacher in the capital city of a tropical dictatorship, he plays neither bridge nor tennis. But he does have a liking for detective stories and for crosswords . . .

And then above all else there's this way of twisting and turning apparently ordinary pieces of information so as to squeeze a hidden meaning out of them, this endless, pernickety *explication de texte* which purports to pierce the story's obscurity but which in fact only sets its wheels in motion . . . What exactly is he supposed to be doing? How can he be sure of finding any bearings in a gallery of distorting mirrors?

It's all there in the opening lines: the city under military patrol, the state of emergency: of course, it's just the lamentably ordinary picture of a police state – but it's also France under the Occupation, with the Flying Squad, the "Resistance" (of café waiters) and even a curious allusion to the "patriotic choice" of "good French [wines] and true." There aren't any words which would give too much away too soon, such as maquis, but could "Hermitage" not be decoded into "La Chartreuse"?

CHAPTER TWENTY-THREE

Ring-file 91

In the middle of the month of January, Salini contacts Patricia again. She can see him at her home in Rue Murillo. He asks her:

"Did he talk to you about this man Chabert?"

"Not that I can recall."

"He told you what he did in the war?"

"Of course . . . but rather vaguely . . . spoke of the Chartreuse . . . nothing very detailed."

Salini sighs.

"It's our only lead . . . no one knows what he's called."

Salini goes home.

He looks up his copy of Balzac's *Le Colonel Chabert* reads

Chabert had two friends, two old comrades-in-arms, one called Boutin who lives with two performing polar bears; and an "Egyptian" (a veteran of the Egyptian Campaign *[of 1802]* called Louis Vergnaud. They're the only ones who recognise and help him, alongside the solicitor Derville (later on).

NOW these three names plus some details appear in

CHAPTERS TWENTY-FOUR & TWENTY-FIVE

Bedside 3

24   Chabert   the hypothesis
     Chabert and   have got hold of proof of
       Louviers's treachery
25   Chabert: *Le Colonel Chabert*
     still has to be found in a cold city or a hot city

Ring-file 92

24/25

How to find Chabert
    Salini re-reads Balzac
    Comes across Derville
           X
        and Y

so Chabert
the film came out in December '43
when "Chabert" joined up

    there were many Chaberts in the Resistance, par-
ticularly after the release of René le Henaff's film.
Chabert is the one who says "I" in the book – the narrator. His name, Veyraud, is mentioned once only.
    Veyraud . . . but there is no character called Veyraud
in Balzac's story
    true, but there are many, including the former Com-
tesse Chabert, who are called Ferraud
    "se non è vero . . ."

CHAPTER TWENTY-SIX

Bedside 3

> The hot city

Blue 3

> That's when he leaves for another tropical country where Chabert (perhaps) is to be found (but not a consul – the Consul was only there because of Stendhal).
> but what?

White 1

> Salini is on the plane. Looks out of the window. Quite something, the way he still gets excited about seeing fields and towns and deserts from so far up, after so many, many travels. Other passengers almost never look.
> Salini puts his mind to the case in hand. What does it all mean

CHAPTER TWENTY-SEVEN

Rhodia 5

> Clues which will enable Salini to discover the "real" truth?
> – Why a book: why would former *résistants*, assuming that they really had picked up Serval, established his

guilt, sentenced and then killed him, why would they
have needed to write novel A? To draw him into a trap?
That's what is said. But if all that had been really true,
Serval would have killed himself.

All that could *also* be true!

Serval really did substitute himself for   in the
Resistance, passed himself off as a hero, etc. Madame
Serval knew. But that's not at all why he was killed.

Blue 4

"Chabert's" "Confessions"
  this confession
  "solves the *enigma*"
  the affair is shelved

Rhodia 5

Madame Serval and her lover wish to get rid of Serval
before he divorces her. They set up a plot whose twists
and motives are unscrambled by Salini from the "mirror-book."

If the corpse is not found, then Madame S. would
not inherit.

If the police find it, then they won't swallow the
hook of the "*résistants*' revenge."

They'll be even less inclined if it is Madame Serval
who provides the lead herself.

Ring-file
96–97

When we began to work out how we might tackle the
murder of Serval, I was reading *La Chartreuse de Parme*.

You know how things are. When something is

on your mind, you find it cropping up everywhere. As soon as you're hungry, you notice restaurants all the time, or if you're under treatment you notice that there's a chemist's every fifteen yards. In a word, I began to see coincidences on almost every page, first of all the *Chartreuse*, then the fact that Fabrice needed forged documents to get to the battle of Waterloo, when Serval actually forged papers himself, and so on.

Ring-file
102

It was that name Chabert which prompted us to use a book as the key to the whole affair . . . Colonel Chabert, who comes back from the dead forty years after . . . But that would have given a direct lead too early on. It was better to find something else – a better-known novel. The Chartreuse made us think of Stendhal, and that's how it all started (Patricia: final explanation)

We hunted through *La Chartreuse de Parme* and other works by Stendhal for elements which could (after a while) be seen as a trail. St Réal, etc.

then we looked for a writer

CHAPTER TWENTY-EIGHT

Ring-file
103

The truth (the "harsh truth," as Stendhal or Danton would have said) is given explicitly in this mysterious manuscript: just as Serval, abetted by his lover Lise, murders the Consul and guarantees his own impunity, so "The Consul," abetted by his lover Patricia, murders Robert Serval. But this truth is displayed only to make it impossible to see. Its laughable obviousness is swallowed up by the cloak of fiction.

Ring-file 99

We met Perec at Zagora, in the southern part of Morocco. One day we went on an outing into the desert with him. Not by camel, obviously enough, nor even in a Landrover, but in an air-conditioned Cadillac. When we drove past that sign, etc.
    Coincidence?

Ring-file
101

THE END
    Salini (to Patricia): Who wrote the book?
    P: A novelist whom we met at   . he is called GP apparently he adores these sorts of problems. We gave him a number of key words, themes, names. It was up to him what he did with them.
    S: You weren't disappointed with the result
    P: I haven't really read the book, just checked

that all the allusions were there. It did not displease me that false trails were laid.

S: But why the title, *53 Days*?

P: It's the time Stendhal took to write *La Chartreuse de Parme*. You didn't know? We talked about that a great deal when we first met. He too wanted to write a book in 53 days. That was actually what gave us the idea of the challenge: to take 53 days to write a novel for which we would supply this and that piece.

In fact, he took a lot longer. We had made allowances for overruns, but in the end we really had to breathe down his neck . . .

Paris–Brisbane–Bressuire
1981–1982

III

DRAFTS

Georges Perec was working on "53 Days" *at the time of his death in March 1982 .*

The first French edition of "53 Days," *published in 1989, consists of two distinct parts:*

  – the uncorrected typescript of chapters 1 to 11 (there were to be 28 chapters in all, 13 in part I, 53 Days, *and 15 in part II,* Un R est un M qui se P le L de la R*).*

  – a set of notes and plans relating both to the chapters in typescript and to those which were left undrafted, though it is not always possible to say for which chapter this or that note was intended. Perec's jottings reflect the chronology of the book's composition and allow us to see his hesitations and changes of mind.

The only alterations made to the typescript chapters by the French editors were corrections of obvious typing and spelling mistakes.

The notes and plans which constitute the other main part of the book consist of a substantial but not exhaustive transcription of the mainly manuscript documents in which all of Perec's drafts and preparatory notes are to be found. These materials are physically distributed amongst several different exercise books, notepads and files. The editors, Harry Mathews and Jacques Roubaud, present these documents in what appears to be the order of their composition.

"In this non-academic edition of an unpublished novel," *the editors wrote,* "it seemed to us appropriate to intercalate between the drafted and undrafted parts of *"53 Days"* a *selection* of passages from the manuscript sources which allow the reader, if he or she so wishes, to follow the probable path of the novel's unfolding."

These passages (Chapters Twelve and Thirteen, concluding Part I of the novel, and Chapters Fourteen to Twenty-Eight, which would have constituted Part II) can all be found in the transcriptions of the preparatory documents (sources are indicated in the margin). The French editors made only minor changes – completing all but the most obvious abbreviations and altering the layout to allow continuous reading.

With the permission of the editors of the French text, I have restored a small number of sentences and one or two passages written in English which were omitted from the preparatory documents in the original edition. A few corrections of readings of Perec's hand were also made prior to translation. Six of the manuscript pages reproduced as facsimiles in the French edition have been exchanged for six other pages which are less dependent on an ability to read French.

In nearly all other respects this edition of "53 Days" is a translation of the text published by Harry Mathews and Jacques Roubaud.

DB

ORANGE EXERCISE BOOK

series:	lager	régal
metalanguage	cab	bac
workings of the book in the book	noël	Léon
Stendhal	émir	rime
a) *Charterhouse of Parma*	as	sa
b) travels in France	amuser	résuma
c) biography	aval	lava
effects of TLO	sac	cas
detective fiction	élime	Emile
personal diary (day by day)	Eton	note
schedule	Erie	Eire
the book is a mirror,etc.	état	tâté
natural palindromes	Eric	cire
anagrams	trace	écart

allows the papers to pile up
cuttings on any subject

"53 Days" is the title of the story (part 1)
which is given to the narrator of part 2
who undertakes to interpret it

2nd part in the 3rd person
       Serval got the manuscript on 16 May

It was slipped under his doormat
the envelope, etc.

Names of the Wandering Jew:
  Buttadeo (Historiæ de Buon compagno da Signa et Guido
    Bonatti)
  Isaak Lakedem (Flanders)
  Juan de Espera en Dios (Spain)
  Ahasuerus

f° 2 recto

incorporation   François Léon Salini
  music
  painting
  gastronomy
  reading matter
  quotations
  allusions
  Life A User's Manual

                        For Oulipo: Stendhal identified
                        For Raymond Queneau: A.H. *tu(é–
                        la mort aux truths)*

The 2nd story is the false exegesis of the 1st
vertigo of explanations without end

at the end the narrator imagines a 3rd story
which would be the contradictory exegesis of the 2 others?

Read *Isabelle* by André Gide.

fº 2 verso

Playing bridge

"To seek in the fertility of his imagination resources against the sterility of history"	(Anonymous preface of *La Conjuration contre Venise* ("Conspiracy against Venice"), Menard & Desenne. Paris, Bibliothèq. Fran. 1821

fº 3 recto

Characters:	Saint Réal = César
Mr Fly (Mosca)	Vichard abbé de St R[éal]
William Vidornaught	Chambéry
Lise	Dispute with Varillas
Robert Serval	Historiographer of Gaston d'Orléans

fº 4 recto

Organisation
Network
Motive

fº 5 recto

4 November to 26 December: 53 days (p. 1370)

fº 5 verso

wearing out
memory
nostalgia
writing

CLUES

lassitude

families
postcards

fº 6 recto

dinner at the Café Anglais (David Beckett)
applauding Rachel on stage
Memories of a tourist

escape

fº 7

Inscription carved on the fronton of the New York GPO
Neither snow nor rain
nor heat nor gloom of night
stays these couriers
from the swift completion
of their appointed rounds

fº 8 recto

In the car they did not talk very much
Very soon, life settled down to a daily rhythm
punctuated by the baker's van, the postman bringing yesterday's
Le Monde and today's *Nouvelle République*, the 7 o'clock bus.
The rest of the time: the sounds of birds, dogs, cows, sheep, the
noise of main roads in the far distance, background noises

_____

The Recluse (*Le Reclus*) is the title of one of the tales
(but Reclus, precisely, is <u>also</u> the name of a geographer)

fº 8 verso

Life of quiet
The woman
her relationship with Serval
with X?

1st part: he
      (told from the point of view of X)
2nd part: I
      (a)   as if it was me GP ⎫
      (b)   as if it were Serval! ⎭   I don't think so

fº 9 recto

Linguistic robot
A character like Slim or Robert Ban
who instead of getting up and saying I'm off cheerio
acts as if he were reciting a pre-ordained routine
And now I'm going to wish you good night and take my leave

fº 9 verso

genres
      nested narratives
      letters
      diary

Character
  Valserre (Serval) family name of the Del Dongos (138 top)

(Dong-maker: bell foundryman?)

f⁰ 10 recto

28 chapters
1st part I to XIII (put chapters as literals: one, two etc.)
2nd part from XIV to XXVIII.
  Proust: A la recherche de l'étang perdu *[In Search of Pond Lost]*
  Stendhal: l'acheteuse de Parme *[The Parma Ham Purchaser]*
  Queneau: exercices de stylet *[Stiletto Exercises]*
  Verne: Le Tour du Monde en quatre-vingt meurtres *[Around the World in Eighty Deaths]*
  About: l'homme à l'oreille cachée *[The Man with the Hidden Ear]*

f⁰ 10 verso

a coded message (p. 36)
to cross the lake on a boat

atmosphere of civil war (submachine-guns
were parked near the French lycée

one day he told how on the day
of his birth his mother had
planted a chestnut tree not
far from a large fountain (50)

f⁰ 11 recto

First chapter
X a teacher in a tropical city
is summoned by his consul
who asks him to investigate the disappearance
of a French novelist living for x years in said city
X only knows this novelist by name, has read 2 or 3 of his books
He learns that the novelist's real name is [Robert Serval *deleted*]
that they were together at school
X accepts the mission entrusted to him
As he walks he calls up his memory
of his school years and the much vaguer remembrance of RS
he came one evening in November, during the study-period
he could scarcely read or write

f⁰ 11 verso

astrology

unlimited confidence in signs foretelling the future (p. 40)

note on bells, page 1386!
bells p. 46
the fat pale face of his brother (Ascanio) p. 46
(Ascanio) is six years older than he is

Vasi barometer-seller 48
    p. 53 he is the one thought to be a seller of barometers
23 planned assassinations of Napoleon 48–49

the terrible news 49

f° 12 verso

the novel is a mirror   The Red . . .
etc.   (St Réal ⟶ St   al
                                                              en
check the epigraph   ⟶ Rénal
references   ST RE AL
                                      STE N AL
                                            (D)

mirror themes
    Alice
    Through a glass darkly (bible?)
    Daily Mirror ⟶ British (ex-British) colony
        (e.g. Seychelles, Mahé?)

4 versions of the same fact

"a crime novel whose centre is the crime novel"
2nd part   Serval gets the ms
        wonders about it
        dies 53 days later
        (yes but what of?)

f° 14verso

notebooks
follow the mirror idea submissively

give titles
    (some enigmatic)
    to the chapters (cf *Tlooth*)

Childhood memories 12–18
    Marolles en Hurepoix
    Bouray
    Lardy

Chamarande
Etréchy
Etampes

Food ration cards

Names of school friends

(*Real Life of Sebastian Knight*)

f° 15 recto

Now and again epigraphs for the chapters

f° 16 recto

2nd part

Serval's death was announced to the press on –
the famous writer had been found in his study
the day before by X
autopsy?
amongst the papers and documents found on his desk
there was a ms of X pages
entitled *53 Days*
the inquest revealed that this ms had not been written
by Serval
that he had received it just under 2 months previously
_____

And it all starts over (in Paris)
except that it all goes in a new direction

Publisher
Friends
Girlfriends
the Detective?

ff 16 verso –
17 recto

	1st part		2nd part
		28	
		27	_____
	1	26	
	2	25	
	3	24	
	4	23	
	5	22	
	6	21	
	7	20	
	8	19	
	9	18	
	10	17	
	11	16	
	12	15	
	13	14	

↑ a novel: a mirror which
you hold aloft to life
(Stendhal)

f⁰ 18 recto

Volume 2 of *Evelyn Innes*, by George Moore, in the Tauchnitz
collection
L'Espèce humaine, by A. de Quatrefages, Bibliothèque Scientifique
Internationale, vol. XXIII, Paris, Germer Baillière et Cie, 1877

Story 1 is told
by someone who sees from a long way off

But story 2

fº 18 verso

If Serval grasps too clearly
that he is unmasked
he'll commit suicide
so mustn't

What has to happen is that the decipherment
of story I forms the investigation of II
leads Salini on the path to
discovery
Serval dies with his secret
Salini pierces it finds the guilty men (X and "the Consul")

all of it corroborated in the last chapter (the "Consul"'s
   confession?)

fº 19 recto

story nº 1 tells a tale
story nº 2 tells a quite different tale
role of 2nd story in the 1st

fº 19 verso

Michel <u>Henri</u>: *Histoire de la Résistance* (1950)
European Resistance Movements
   Liège 1960 Pergamon
   Milan 64
Aron, *Histoire de la Libération de la France.* Fayard, 1959
Amouroux, *La Vie des Français sous l'occupation*
Michel   D802   A2
(??)   D802   E915
Liège
Milan

Chambard   D802
les maquis   F8C 4413
Dauk   D802 F8028
Bird *The Secret Battalion* (Haute Savoie)
        D762
Ency PN543

f⁰ 20 recto

6 In search of a typist
On rereading the ms once again I became convinced that it had
been typed professionally

14 the disappearance
15 Investigations
16 Return to book: *un r est un
    m* . . .
17 Stendhal
18 the Chartreuse
19 the Commando
20 The cave
21 who what how where
22 Chabert and Balzac
23 the cold trail

24 the hot trail
25 A man called Derville
26 the Confession

27
28 Epilogue the harsh truth

Wine label stuck on to cover of the Orange Exercise Book

RHODIA NOTEPAD

f° 4

how did Serval's comrades
know that he betrayed them
that he had been turned around

How do they let Serval know that they know
(supposing that they do)

The <u>arrival</u> of the ms has to be explained
as well as Serval's behaviour
on the eve of his disappearance

Where was he coming from
where was he going
what traces did he leave

One character will be called BAUTZEN (the only
battle in which Stendhal really took part)

"give one's horse to one's father" (Fabrice deprived of his horse
by ex-lieutenant Robert

Stendhal criticism   Brombert
                      McWatters *Stendhal and England*
                                Liverpool University Press 1976
                                Inaugural Lecture Series

f⁰ s

53 Days

A   the detective novel
B   provides clues to explain
C   incorrectly

Start from C
Mme Serval and her lover wish to get rid of Serval before he divorces her. They set up a plot whose twists and motives are unscrambled by Salini from the "mirror-book."
If the corpse is not found, Mme Serval would not inherit.
If the police find it, they won't swallow the hook of the *"résistant's* revenge."
They'll be even less inclined if it is Mme Serval who provides the lead herself.

Clues which will enable Serval [Salini]to discover the "real" truth?
– Why a book: why would former *résistants,* assuming that they really had picked up Serval, established his guilt, sentenced and then killed him, why would they have needed to write novel A? To draw him into a trap? That's what is said. But if all that had been really true, Serval would have killed himself.
All that could <u>also</u> be true!!
Serval really did substitute himself for   in the Resistance, passed himself off as a hero, etc. Madame Serval knew. But that's not at all why he was killed.

	32
In fact C can be very short: just a curtain	64
a final reversal	128
	256
Has Serval read story A? Obviously not	+12

There is a revolver in the glove-box: Serval's. No fingerprints.

KC	JL	Cr	53	"53"
2	34	36	70	126
	Part I			Part II

	72			142
		142		268

f 7

53 Days: programme

<blockquote>+ name   Lise
+ etc.   apparent</blockquote>

Apart from the name "Serval" there's absolutely no connection between the story told in A and the disappearance of the businessman Serval.

Salini supposes that the story *53 Days* has been sent to Serval to engage the process which leads to his death (in any case, his disappearance)

What is known about Serval: Resistance hero
                                 politician (centre)
                                 wealthy businessman
                                 His private life
                                         Divorce proceedings   not definite
                                       Enquiry on his wife   often at
                                                           spas
Not a slip-up anywhere   poor health
maybe a little one in the history of the Resistance?

<u>SO</u> all you can do is go back to the story

The 1st clue: *Un R est un M qui se p le l d'un C*
  after groping

Salini discovers   Stendhal→Chartreuse→Grenoble
                    St Réal →Chambéry
                    The *Chartreuse*
Now it was <u>precisely</u> in the Chartreuse that some of Serval's
    actions in the Resistance took place.

<u>whence</u> the idea of a coded story
        of a mirror story
        the decipherment of which would provide the key to the
            mystery.

f⁰ 8

Story A

Serval disappears
The police and his Consul investigate: nothing
The Consul entrusts to X an examination of the suitcase found in
    the boot of Serval's abandoned car.
Then to investigate
X's investigation: in fact, he follows the path prepared for him by
Serval (and by his mistress, the Consul's ex-girlfriend)

political false trail

Serval and Lise (?) have to swindle the Consul and X together

Story B

in a way, said Salini, this affair exactly resembles the one described
in the novel called *53 Days*. Someone called Serval has disappeared,
his car has been found, and in his car a suitcase full of papers. The
enquiry produces no result

and, just as, in the novel, the Consul asks X to study the notes made by Serval for his book, you are asking me to conduct an investigation on the basis of a novel. If you pursue the analogy, you could expect it to be Serval who set it all up, you will be the next victim and I will be the false culprit . . .

f[0] 9

BENSABIR	ABBEINRS	BRASBIEN
SBARINEB	RABBEINS	BRABESIN
	BIRABENS	BARNEBIS
		BIRNABES

Examples
    everything has to be reversed

story A	Serval not to be found; in fact he manages to get X charged with the murder of the Consul	
"real"	Serval is not to be found; in fact the Consul and X have murdered him	
	whence: who is the Consul	BABIRENS
	who is X	BRIBESNA
		SERBABIN
story A	Serval is a pseudonym	SERBBIAN
real	Serval had a pseudonym in the Resistance	NIBARBES
		ERABBINS
Question: who wrote story A?		ABBERINS
		SABBERIN
Why the hot town		BERISBAN

    and the cold town (Gotterdam) –
    [Götterdämmerung – got it damn wrong]

In story A   X (must find a name for him quickly)
                  discovers a (false) truth by picking through Serval's
                  manuscripts. In fact he has been "flushed" (flush card)
                  by Serval

In "real" B, Salini uncovers "the" (false?) truth
                  from story A

Example: The nested novel is called the crypt
            This name suggests
                                a hidden meaning
                                a cave
Serval's corpse (for instance) will be found in a cave in the
Chartreuse mountains

f^o *II*

Story A: X works on documents
            found in a case
            in Serval's car (abandoned?)

real: case (with ms of 53 D) in Serval's car

story A: history of the Red Hand, political explanation soon
            proved wrong by X

"real":   Resistance history
                confirmed by Salini

semantic or logical ANTONYMS

Big questions
    Sequence of traps into which X falls
penultimate chapter, end: X discovers, at a particular place that
has been sought virtually since the start, not Serval's but the
Consul's corpse

last chapter begins

> the police came to arrest me next day at dawn
> the Consul, being dead, obviously could not corroborate my
> statements
> On the other hand FIND FOUR CLUES MAKING A
> CHAIN
> a) establishing a motive
> b) destroying every possible alibi
> c) leaving a signature (weapons, fingerprints)
> d) providing a witness

An element from the "real" story
should moreover match
each of these clues

f° 13

Story A	age 20 in 44
entitled 53 *Days*	for instance
when Salini mentions it he writes	the "real" story could
"53 *Days*"	take place in 70
The "real" investigation	
leads Salini to identify as the	so aged 46
culprits two former résistants from	46 + 24 = 70
the Serval (Béraud) ring – "the	born in 24 = 46 in 70
Consul"(?)	(how old is Salini in 70?)
and "X" (?)	(not really important)
("the Consul" is Mme Serval's	
lover)	
But that's where the mystification	born in 24
begins	58 in
In 80, there are no survivors of the	82
affair	

Salini's question to Lise: What if I hadn't found the answer?

Reply: Impossible
            the book really was the only "cue" *[sic]*

        and the Mirror held aloft
        could not but come to mind
        because of all the occurrences of mirrors
        in the story
Mirror, glass, Miror, Spiegel, 1 per page! (or per 2 pages!)

reflection   bird: kookaburra (laughing bird)
image

TITLE OF THE 2ND PART
            Un R est un M qui se P le L de la R

in between the last two pages of the typescript
was a strip of paper bearing
this mysterious formula
        Un R est un M qui se P le L de la R

f° 15

what sort of thing might Béraud (Serval) have done during the
Resistance
Example: the head of the Chambéry Gestapo (Lenoir
                    arrested, executed Béraud and took on his identity
                    in 44)

                    as a member of the Paramilitaries
                    infiltrated a resistance group
                    betrays them all
                    manages to be the only survivor "by a miracle"
                    (but 4 return from the camps)

                    no plastic surgery PLEASE!

f⁰ 19

Problem of suspects

In story A there must be suspicions cast over this one or that

f⁰ 20

Salini hunts for Serval's "real"
classmates
then those who did military service with him
(none left???)
Yes still some
but from the 2nd maquis
CAREFUL: GET TO BOTTOM OF THIS

Salini's reasoning   cf. 7 September 1
        53 Days is the inverted mirror of reality
        in *The Crypt* the pseudonym and the hero are identical
        whence in "reality"
        the pseudonym is not (the) a hero (a man of heroic actions)
        but the opposite: *a traitor*

f⁰ 22

53 Days

Write story A in the 1st person

On 15 May, for the Xth anniversary of Independence . . .

There were still two armoured cars on
guard when I passed in front of the Lycée
Français
An officer casually examined my papers
another searched me before letting me into
the Consul's residence

rather, in a bar cf.
W: GW's
interview with
Apfelstahl

You will forgive me these nuisances, the Consul said, asking me
to sit down

Lise, when X sees her for the 2nd or 3rd time
pretends to recall Y
a man "who might know something"
(in fact it's Serval himself
who hardly needs any make-up

f°25

Must soon find
the characters and plot
of *The Crypt*
and the title, places, characters
and plot of the novel nested
in it
must also quickly decide
    1 – what else there is in the suitcase
    2 – what else we know about Serval
    3 – X is supposed to go to Serval's place
        but actually goes to the Consul's?

he finds Lise's
address in Serval's
notebook

The Consul gives X the task of investigating
he's off to Paris for 2 months

X only sees him again when he's dead
thinking he was going to Serval's he went to the Consul's and
left fingerprints

he went out with the *acheteuse de Parme*
not realizing she was the Consul's mistress
(even less that she was the mistress of Serval
concocting the Consul's murder with him!)

He calls on Lise. She is there
beginning of chapter: I no longer know exactly when it was that I
        realized that I had really and truly fallen in love with Lise
        Nor why (what had attracted me first, what had "crystallized"
He invites her out to dinner
they don't sleep together
she is charming but distant

One day he rings her to tell her. Not in. Rushes round.
Finds the Consul dead. Is arrested next day.

f⁰ 26

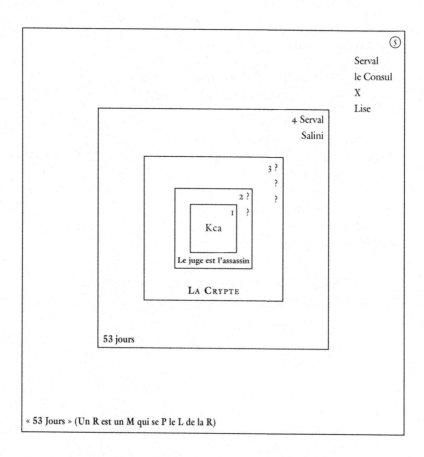

Rhodia Notepad, folio 26: Nested narratives

f° 27

the magistrate is the murderer
A knows that B killed C with utter
   impunity
he kills D in such a way that B
is inexorably accused of the crime

in novel, told in a few pages
it concerns a novel where

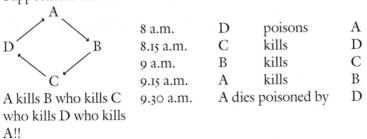

D
   ↗   ↘
2 A   C←B

4 A– C→B

5 A ————→B
3 A←------B
        ↗ "Espionage"
1   The Koala Case Mystery ⟋ "JUSTICE"
2 A kills D so that B who killed C is accused (The Magistrate is
   the Murderer)
3 A disappears   (The Crypt)   VENGEANCE
4 A kills B whilst having C accused of it
             (53 Days)   PASSION
5 A is killed   (quotation marks or "53 Days")
                                     INTEREST

Suppositions for 3:   A pretends that he has been killed by B
                      (*The Tooth and the Nail*) (Bill Ballinger)
                      (vengeance, inheritance?)

Suppositions for 1:

A
  ↗   ↘
D   B
  ↘   ↙
   C
A kills B who kills C
who kills D who kills
A!!

8 a.m.	D	poisons	A
8.15 a.m.	C	kills	D
9 a.m.	B	kills	C
9.15 a.m.	A	kills	B
9.30 a.m.	A dies poisoned by		D

f° 34

1st story   Each time, as in the affair I had to deal with, an essen-
             tial clue seemed to be provided by reading a detective
             novel

2nd story   sentences such as "each time, as in the affair I had to
            deal with, an essential clue seemed to be provided by
            reading a detective novel" obviously took on a quite
            special meaning for Salini
            It was as if someone wanted to <u>oblige</u> him to find the
            truth in *53 Days*

f° 47

                                    URGENT QUESTION

Procedures
                                    Salini's reactions on receiving
                                    the book?

A clue in Koala Case
gives an idea of the murder in *The*
Magistrate is the Murderer   mechanics of the murder
                                    and <u>especially</u>
this idea or clue helps   THE NEED (other than
Serval with *The Crypt*   literary) for such a scenario
                                    it's of no importance at the level
                                    of
X reading *The Crypt* finds in   the <u>other</u> stories
Serval's deduction from that   since they turn out to be
idea a clue to explain Serval's   fictions but the 5th must have
"disappearance" (but is wrong)   a semblance of plausibility

Salini in reading *53 Days*
reinterprets the whole set of
elements

In practice
each time I <u>place</u> a detail or clue
at one level
think through the consequences
in the machinery of *The Crypt*

ditto   of 53 D
ditto   of "53 D"

so: body must be found
        justify Serval's murder
        shift suspicion away from
        Mme Serval

so provide an
        explanation satisfactory
        enough not to make you
        want to go and dig around
        elsewhere
        well precisely the idea of an
        old *résistant*'s revenge

the basic idea of OULIPo work is to study and practice. — 36
what we called CONSTRAINTS
The word itself may be not the proper one
because it implies the idea of an ordeal or restraint
which is not exactly at all what we intend to
create . In a way we want to give FREEDOM thal'n CREATIVITY
to writers, but we think that what is called FREEDOM or CRE
in writing is not obtained by chance but through
a specific work

May be I could make myself more clear
with the following aphorisms used by us to
describe our project
For instance one of us said
An oulyian is a rat who builts up the labyrinth
from which he will later want to go out

or Calvino explains
An oulyian writer is like a hurdler sprinter who
runs faster when there are hurdles on the track

We also said : oulyian is a non-jourdainian prosodist
M'jourdain writes prose without knowing it
and we want to write prose knowing what we are doing

I can explain also like this
Oulyian it acts towards language
like a child towards an alarm clock
when you present him duild an al cl
he will undo it in order to know how it
works . Ou does the same with language

A page of Perec's notes for a lecture given in Australia, written in the
Rhodia Notepad

BLUE EXERCISE BOOK

f⁰ 1 verso

what
in this whole story
really "meant"
anything
save the absurd
situation
where the books seems
to prefigure
the investigation
a manuscript found in a car
a Serval gone missing . . .

Where to begin

f⁰ 2 recto

Main problems to solve

In *"53 Days"* ("Un R est un M . . .")
how does the reading of *53 Days*
lead Salini to the "path of the truth"

1   With the help of Patricia and the official
    investigators he identifies all the allusions
    concerning Serval. There aren't that many
    but there are some all the same

which are precise and sometimes strange
for instance the tie
Where to begin?

2   He thinks he has a "hot country" lead, which leads nowhere
very precise. He rules it out without going there.

3   same thing for the "cold country" lead

4   he buckles down to "un r est un m" etc. . . .
first responds to the multiplicity of "Mirrors"
so: an R is a mirror which
he clicks

5   That puts him straight on to Stendhal, St Réal
everything fits
everything seems to take on a meaning
but which?
It's the *Chartreuse* which is being designated

6   so the Chartreuse affair is gone over again

f⁰ 3 recto

7   witnesses to find

8   Places to locate

9   On that score also the book comes to his rescue
the place is a crypt, id est a cave

10   The corpse is found

11   So that really was it

12   YES but how, who, why

13   Hypothesis provided by the "mirror book"
     Serval in the book is "hero and pseudonym"
         That means Serval-pseudonym (Louviers) is not a hero!
         but a traitor

14   Who can know that?
         "the Consul"?
         "the teacher-narrator"?

15   That's when he leaves once more for a different tropical country where Chabert (perhaps) is to be found
     not a Consul (the Consul was only there because of Stendhal)
     but what?
     businessman? academic?
     Artist (why?)
     ?

f⁰ 4 recto

16   So he finds Chabert
     once more thanks to clues
     from the book
         for instance a character called Cat-ours
         (*chat*-bear *[pronounce*: shaber, "*Chabert*"])
         or
         a feature discovered when studying the biography of the *résistant*
         alias Chabert
         and found in the book
         (not previously suspected)

a character called Boutin who might have taken the pseudonym of Chabert because of the film (Boutin is another one of Balzac's characters in *Le Colonel Chabert*)

17 "Chabert's" "confession"

18 This confession
    "solves the enigma"
    the affair is shelved

19 Epilogue
    "true truth"
    the truth, the harsh truth

f° 10 verso

Clues

The 1st quality of a clue
is its presence

the second is its absence

once again the clue functions in the manner of a crossword
definition
        obscure as long as its clue-status is unrevealed
        transparent when it finally finds its place in the reverse-order
        reasoning of the crime writer

generalization of the clue
        seduction
        challenge
        plausibility

f⁰ 23 verso

The narrator must find clues
<u>in</u> the book
these clues must
incite him to take certain
actions which for him will be
fatal
he'll not understand
until after

e.g.   the Italian delicatessen ⟶ meeting Lise
        Lise chooses a <u>clue</u> restaurant (for example, in *The Crypt*,
                            question of a painting which
                            the Narrator sees in this
                            restaurant)

f⁰ 24 recto

		"53 Days"
53 Days		"Un R est un M qui se P le L de la R"
		14
		15 53 Days manuscript full of deletions, additions, repetitions, corrections, etc.
		16
		17
		18
6	looking for a typist	19
7		20
8		21
9		22
10		23

f⁰ 30 recto

The 4 clues which will do for the narrator

D – He will be in Lise's company (motive)

E – His fingerprints will be on the gun

F – A witness sees him go into the
      Consul's at the time of the murder
      and come out looking crazy!

D

f⁰ 31 recto

Twelfth Chapter

Narrator more and more in love with Lise

at the same time
the "frightening thought"
forms in his mind: that the Consul
killed Serval and is in the process of pinning
the crime on him
It's an intuition,   the book contains no hidden
no real clue   truth it was just a decoy, a
      or else the revolver?   pretext

Lise telephones him in a panic
he dashes round in a taxi to her place
rings the bell.
The door is open
he hears a shot
rushes up to the bedroom
and discovers the Consul's corpse!

f° 32 recto

Thirteenth Chapter

the police came to arrest me next day
at five in the morning.

I was expecting it
and had not tried to flee.

I don't know exactly how they managed it
but I know that I have no chance.
"They," I suppose, are Lise
and Serval who faked his own disappearance
and planned the crime which I would inexorably
appear to have committed

I'm sure my fingerprints
are on the revolver
and that someone saw me coming out
looking dazed and in a total panic

all night long I have been
thinking the affair over   Reconstruction of the affair just
Why choose me, etc.   as the book (*The Crypt*) led the
                                narrator's investigation

Of course I'll show this diary to the Grianta
police
but I'm not under any illusions

f° 36 verso

1 2 3 4 5 6 7 8 9 10 11 12 13 14 15 16 17 18
U N R O M A N E S T U N M I R O I R
N E L E L O N G D E L A R O U T E

19 20 21 22 23 24 25 26 27 28

Q U I S E P R O M E   = 45

45 verso

The final Question (sic) is: what   – Places
is the novel of which *53 Days* is   – Names
the 1st part?   – Facts
                                       Allegory of the Truth
                                       the missing link
                                             Hellige Luise

loose leaves slipped into the blue exercise book

Pseudonyms

	Foulques	Correspondence	558
	Firmin (Alex. de)	Correspondence	826
	Firmin (L. de)		833
	Florise		767
	Alex. Clapier		789 1019
	General Cok		678
×	Collière R.		633

Chalet Ch	793	
✶ ~~Chamier~~	802	
Charbonel (Charles)	795	
Chapart	619	
Chapelain	691	
Chappuis (Alex.)	786	
Champel	777 779	
× Chapuis	711	
Carré	964	
Chevallet J A	584	
Chomette Ch	686	
✶ ~~The Chinaman~~	65 804 1087 1438	
Aubertin	890 etc.	
Aubier	808	
✶ ~~Aubry~~	1041	
Auguste	1065	
✶ ~~Cl. Turpin~~	341 PTO	

Robert	937		Romorantin 618
Serin	688		
✶ ~~Smith and Co~~	1055		
Sorbon	568		
× Souchevort	667		
× Tavistock	918 1401		
Terré	766		
× Thermin Victor	799		
Thine	574		
Roux	694		
O Lani	850 etc.		
× Lanvallère	548		
Larridon	345		
× Lauzanne	806		
Mingrot (?)	781		
Lecœur			
Gelé			
Giuseppe			
Des Chapons			

Tourte	1011
Toricelli	925
Curzay, Marquis of	872
Curiosité	927
Desu (César)	690

NOTEPAD ON THE BEDSIDE SHELF

f⁰ 2

Epigraph: Snow
as a proof
sheet

14: Serval's disappearance: elements of the investigation
Salini's mission

15: Salini reads *53 Days*, rereads it once, twice 3 times 4 times.
He doesn't know what to do
with Madame Serval he lists the allusions to Serval in
53 Days etc.

16: Grianta? Etampes? Names of people,places,etc.?

17: Where to begin: "un r est un m"
attempts; commentaries on the attempts

18: The frequency of the word mirror and its cognates.
Solution found

19: Saint Réal

20: the book is given to a Stendhal expert
list of allusions to *La Chartreuse de Parme*

21: so CDP = la Chartreuse
the past in the Resistance: Paris. Lyon. Grenoble
correspondences in the novel (letter box, coded messages)

22:   "the Chartreuse affair". The Commando explanation of
the II changed words

23:   The Cave: discovery of corpse!

fº 3

24:   Chabert   the hypothesis
                   Chabert and   have got hold of proof
      of Louviers's treachery

25:   Chabert: *Le Colonel Chabert*
      still has to be found in a cold city or a hot city
      a man called   , . . . or Ferraud (<u>the</u> Narrator!)

26:   The hot city

27:   the confession of Ferraud. Murder made public, etc.

28:   The truth   the harsh truth
      Perec   And here he is on the job etc. (Roussel)

WHITE EXERCISE BOOK

f⁰ 1

Model for Salini

Present tense

Very direct

Salini is on the plane. Looks out of the window.
Quite something, the way he still
gets excited about seeing
fields and towns and deserts from so far up,
after so many, many travels. Other passengers almost never look.
Salini puts his mind to the case in hand. What does it all mean

NOTES ON THE DRAFTED CHAPTERS

f⁰ 1

Allusions to Serval-Louviers in *53 Days*
– Born at Rouen without being of Norman stock
– Jaguar (red for Serval-Réal, black for Serval-Louviers)
– Veulle-les-Roses
–

–

– hates champagne (like Einar Svendsen)
– Has a villa at Le Pecq (like Fly) p. 45
– Likes walking-sticks
– Wife's maiden name: Carpenter

f⁰ 2

the title: *53 Days*: the time Stendhal took to write *La Chartreuse de Parme*

page 3*: 15 May
(the postcard Timbuktoo 52 days is perhaps an allusion)
in fact some authorities say 52 days instead of 53. In fact if Stendhal began on   in the morning and finished on   in the evening, then he really did take 53 days.
reporter p. 28

*Of the original typescript.

page 3	Cularo (amongst others, *Correspondence* p. 711 (Pléiade); 10 lines in the index p. 1513
	Grianta
page 4	zabaglione
page 5	Monférine
page 6	"Il pleut sur le lac de Côme"
page 7	Beatrix
	Lescale
	Feder
page 8	Consul in a small town in Italy
page 9	"Rouge"
page 10	Veal cutlet with spinach cf. *Journal* p. 531 12 August 1804
page 11	Réal St Crozet (cf. also 54)
page 13	Charlier
	red Jaguar (as opposed to Serval's black Jaguar)
	Alzire
page 16	15 5 97
page 17	The Marquis (*Lemarquis*) professed
	a little man, etc.
	Virgil to be copied
page 18	Chamier
	Bombet milliner
	Verrières (*The Red*)
page 19	Dominique
	Salviati
	Pedrotti and Pedrocchi (confusion at the beginning of *La Chartreuse*)
	Rue des Vieux-Jésuites
page 20	Charbonel
p. 21	Borroni
	Ariosto
	Bédollière (the critic) + Fabrice getting 5 first prizes p. 35
[22]	Ambroise Dupont
	Auguste Dupouy

Aubry pseudonym + character at Waterloo (71 ss.)
Pierrette Lenoir = Pietranera
Crocodile??
Duboin
Dufour
Lanvallère

f° 3

page 23   soles and laces cf. Lt. Robert
    24   Turpin
         Collière
         Levasseur
         Chapuis
         Jay art teacher
         "pale fat face" Ascanio p. 46
         "noise of silence" cf.' Fabrice at Waterloo p. 1389
                  p. 25 coded messages: cf. the Marquis and
                      his elder son in chapter 1
    26   "star of the sixth" = "*as de sa khagne*" = Ascagne
         given and gotten . . . quotation p. 34
         way of learning to read p. 34
    27   Fabrice soon found the mess wagon → Serval soon
         found the Marktendörin
         (Marketenderin = mess wagon, camp-follower
         Gestriglebend: living yesterday(!)
    28   The Giletti Affair: it was because he killed Giletti the
             actor that Fabrice del Dongo is thrown into jail
         The corpse had one eye open: cf. first corpse seen by
             Fabrice at Waterloo + Vichard
         52 days cf. title
    29
    30

31 Blackstone =pietranera
!!! Derville is the fictitious name of Sophie Boulon the
    friend of Pauline Beyle (wife of Casimir Gauthier)
32 Barrett is the name under which Stendhal published his
    letters on Haydn, *paramour* cf. opening of *La Char-
    treuse.*
33 The Chinaman is one of Stendhal's most frequent pseud-
    onyms
    Jacobson banker
    Van Proet
    Stanley Dahlström
    Dept. of Transport cf. Crozet
    Hazlitt: *Characters of Shakespeare's Plays*
34 César Vichard, real name of Abbé de Saint-Réal, born at
    Moutiers
    Devaux, name of Henri Beyle's predecessor as consul at
    Civitavecchia
35 Smolensk, Brunswick, Vienna: Henri Beyle stayed in
    these 3 towns
36 Périer-Lagrange name of Henri Beyle's sister (one of his
    chief correspondents)
37 CDP 411.38 CDP: *Chartreuse de Parme* 4.11.38 date on
    which Stendhal began the book
39 Hôtel de Nantes: last home of Henri Beyle in Paris
    Boulot: name of the dead hussar whose clothes Fabrice
    takes at Waterloo
    223: 22 March 19 hrs date and time of the apoplectic fit
    that killed Henri Beyle.

f⁰ 4

42 b . . . for *bougre* ("bugger"), frequent in Stendhal
43 Smith and Co: pseudonym used by Stendhal for letters
    (in English) to Adolphe de Mareste (31 XII 1820)

44 in the description of the room: red and black, pink and
      green
    Angèle, Saint-Séverin, Taxi = Angelina
      Sanseverina-Taxis
    Fly: Mosca ("fly" in Italian)
    Hôtel de Bourgogne: Henri Beyle's first home in Paris
48 Marhenbey read MARie HENri BEYle.
    Triestine police
49 Lauzanne Pseudonym of Stendhal
    Tavistock   „
    Thermin
    Souchevort
    16.1 (1782) Birth of Henri Beyle, who lived 4 days (one
      year before Henri Beyle/Stendhal)
50 Chappuis another of Stendhal's pseudonyms
    Gelé   „
    Julien Labbé Julien Sorel? or l'Abbé de Saint-Réal
51 23 4 184259 Stendhal died on 23.3.1842 at the age of
      59
    Hartz instead of Hertz: cf. 369, 481 (descent into the
    Dorothea mineshaft, check De l'Amour)
55 St Margaret's St Chartreuse p.94
    Bender (Binder)   head of Milan police p. 101 ss
56 Groenjäger   the Green Hunter
    Bayard: Fabrice takes refuge at Romagnano where
      Bayard was killed
    Gagliani, Galignani: another one of Stendhal's
      confusions letter N° 646 Note p.1401 Correspondence
58 English Mail: "Le Courrier anglais"
62 Disinvoltura p.112
    St Férant   cf. Ferrante p. 124
    Sfondrata   p. 119
    Landriani   p. 128 (archbishop of Parma)
    Sorezana   p. 111
    Scagliola   p. 125
    Bentivoglio   p. 130 (one of Raversi's friends)
    Contarini   p. 127

63   Voi mi avete lasciatto p. 1241 letter from Angela
      Pietragrua
65   Marginalia
67   Chlemm p. 119
      Colomb   friend and executor of Henri Beyle.

f° 5

68   Chekina   *Chartreuse* p. 157 one of Sanseverina's
      chambermaids
72   Monitor   cf. *Le Moniteur* newspaper often read by
                 Stendhal
      Misène   on 12 January 1832 Henri Beyle buys a bust
                 of Tiberius found by a peasant at Miseno +
                 Chartreuse p. 144
      Antoine Berthet: model for Julien Sorel
      Don Carlos + quotation: Saint-Réal, preface
74   Bust of Tiberius *Chartreuse* p. 144
      "Trecuzrah" anagram of Chartreuz
76   So less than a month after arriving opening of chapter
      eight of *La Chartreuse* 160
      Brighella: actor who thrashes Giletti the lover of
      Marietta p. 162

78–79   *Chartreuse* p. 26 in a big Milan café, the painter
         Gros draws a caricature representing the Archduke of
         Austria: a soldier . . . "Legros," "Milan," "wheat," and
         the knife-thrust crop up in *53 Days*
         Henri Legros [*"the fat one"*] could also designate Henri
         Beyle (who was notoriously fat)
79   Macklin cf. *Journal intime* pp. 1415, 1416, 1417
         An optician in Menaggio called Alesi: Fabrice del
         Dongo takes the passport of his friend Vasi, a barome-
         ter-seller at Menaggio *La Chartreuse* p. 50
         Waterloo is obviously chosen because of Fabrice del
         Dongo's episode at Waterloo

Soltykoff *Correspondence* 662, 675

Apraxine (Apraksin) (palace) 660 *Correspondence*

80 A grammar of the Malayan language by W. Marsden *Correspondence* note p. 1386

81 Shepherd name which Henri Beyle used to refer to La Bergerie. *Correspondence* p. 518, 822, etc.

Hang Puah book by Marsden which Henri Beyle mentions to Louis Crozet *Correspondence* p. 829

Abe Blanes: l'Abbé Blanès, astronomy enthusiast, vicar of Grianta, whom Fabrice sees again at the end of chapter 8 (pp. 170 fl)

82 Charlotte Knabelhuber: Henri Beyle's mistress at Brunswick *Oeuvres intimes* 875 etc.

f° 6

84 cf. 2nd sentence of chapter 9 of *La Chartreuse*: I found it hard to get to sleep

88 Ghita: name of Abbé Blanès's old servant *Chartreuse de Parme* p.178

Allard-Duplantier cousins of Stendhal

Lusinge name Stendhal gave to his friend Mareste in *Souvenirs d'egotisme*

Mounier childhood friend of Stendhal, director of police in 1816

Affó name of a Parma librarian, author of a life of Parmigianino p. 645 (and not 646 as said Pléiade)

89 Fiscal Rassi cf. *La Chartreuse* p.113 and tons of others, enemy of Mosca, chief judge of Parma

Mortaretti little mortars (bangers in fact) let off when the blessed sacrament is processed p. 177

93 I'll be killed if etc. Pléiade p. 182 (just after the start of the tenth chapter)

97 Saint-Aulaire French Ambassador to Rome at the time of Henri Beyle

Delmont: del Monte: vice consul at Ancona

Levasseur: Henri Beyle's successor at Trieste

99 black and yellow striped barriers (Austrian border):
p. 198

100 Was I going to lose my head at well past forty-five, and
have a fling that would make a cadet blush
(cf. Mosca in love: Pléiade p. 115)
Mathilde: allusion to Mathilde de la Môle (or to
Metilde)

102 John Bull: Mosca uses the expression twice in chapter 10
(p. 186)

103 Spielberg: cf. the prison (e.g. p. 184 or chapter 9
p. 181)
Riva: I have the 4 Riva brothers on my heels p. 182
Alari: my cousin the good count Alari p. 182

104 Kolorno cf. chapter 11 p.193 Colorno: the Versailles of the
princes of Parma

105 1st sentence cf. "all that was but a mirage and vanishes in
the austere light of reality" p. 189

108 the same anecdote is told by Fabrice del Dongo p. 186
concerning the Farnese (himself) and the Sforza (the
Duke of Milan)

109 Manzi and Bucci 2 friends of Henri Beyle at
Civitavecchia, with whom he did some excavating
(Pléiade p. 1417 n)
the whole story of the false Kaaba is only there to bring
in the words Black Stone (Pietranera = la
Sanseverina)

111 Sakka cf. Sacca p. 203 (country house where Ludovic
takes la Sanseverina)

112 SHETLAND: anagram of Stendhal (the choice of the
pseudonym "Stendhal" has been ascribed to Henri
Beyle's love of Scotland)

114 episode on stolen medals Pléiade p. 193 (!!! the Author
recommends it!!)

115 Fabian D Donaldson FAB. D. DON (GO) cf. p. 199 all
(RICE) (el)
his linen marked FD

BLACK RING-FILE

That's about it. You could also say that Rouard equals
Mirouet, especially if you take their first names into account:
Mirouet's is André, Rouard's is Rémi (it's there in *The Crypt*, but,
oddly, only once).

and | RÉMIROU | et
RÉMIROU | ard

None of these elements allows me to go any further, or to
try to imagine who else could have pulled it off. On reflection,
practically everybody could have done it, I mean, any petty port
official at Grianta, or a customs officer, or the director of the harbour police, or a couple of crane drivers in cahoots with the container ship's lading officer (because of the heat, ships are loaded
at night). Not to mention the few days when the statue was in
a warehouse at the dockside at Grianta. There was nothing to
prevent the Ambassador, for instance, from having the artic (the
embassy truck-trailer) making a detour on its way from Castellum
Acridium to Grianta. Etc., etc., etc.

So between 17 December 1979, when it was unearthed, and
3 March 1980, when the deception was discovered, three score
and more different people were in a position to get hold of it (the
statue of Diocletian). It would certainly have been easier to do
that than to pin the theft on Mirouet.

I am horribly disappointed. I expected Serval's book to give me
a clear sign, something that lifted the veil clearly and unambiguously on the real culprit, on the man who, when he knew he was
uncovered, had no option but murder!

I don't know what the time was when I woke up in a start. The
bed was soaked in sweat: the truth, the luminous and fearful,
transparent and awful truth had just struck me.

f° 2   B

Mirouet had been manipulated from start to finish, not by the BH (as he must also have told Serval), but by the Consul (and so my mysterious interlocutor had not been lying). In the process of cross-checking, Serval found proof of the Consul's guilt. And that is where the Machiavellian cunning of the whole thing comes into daylight at last: Serval encrypts this manifestly dangerous truth in an unfinished detective story which he gets the Consul himself to read.

The Consul quickly grasps that
he is being blackmailed directly: unless he complies, the book's ending will be so cast as to put the only too obvious culprit, Rouard-Mirouet, in the clear.

f° 3

Frightening thoughts
        The Diocletian affair has left only tiny traces in *The Crypt*, and they are practically impossible to interpret,

– Arethusa = a nymph turned into a spring = nymphaeum and
    fountain.
– DiMagalco = acronym of the tetrarchy.
– MCB 1000 S =
– RAPR =

you could add ROUARD = MIROUET, especially if you take R's first name into account (given once only)

$$\text{AND} \quad \boxed{\begin{array}{l}\text{REMIROU} \\ \text{REMIROU}\end{array}} \quad \begin{array}{l}\text{ET} \\ \text{ARD}\end{array}$$

And that's all. Not enough to pin guilt on anyone.

        I went to bed early, Couldn't get to sleep. Around 10.00 p.m. the transparent, awful truth came to me:

Mirouet was manipulated
not by the BH as he says to Serval
but by the Consul
        (as the BH told me)
Serval has proof of the Consul's guilt
He allows the latter to know it by showing him
        his book <u>without an ending</u>: the dénouement would show
        the consul's guilt. "<u>Unless</u> allowed to prove [*illegible*]
Why? Because he has big
    financial problems (gambling debts)

*f*⁰ 4

Frightening thoughts

pp. 14–16
        A set-up by Serval
        to blackmail the Consul

OR

        a comedy
        scripted by the Consul so as
        to murder Serval and steal
        his manuscript, which
        proves that the Consul
                did it.
        He destroys the ending
        the "real proof"
        so Lise would have to be an accomplice!

*f*⁰ 6

At first glance
you can't see what connection there is

between the theft of a statue
weighing several tons
and desert outings

Nonetheless, it is obvious
that the Consul is one of the few people
in a sufficiently powerful position
to think up, carry out and get away with
a crime of that kind

But, in that case
why the devil should
Serval
when he discovers the truth
have it read specifically
by the culprit himself

It's absolute madness!

Or is it the high point
of his cunning
or more exactly
a blackmail operation

What I mean is: Serval
has the Consul read his book.
That says: if this book comes out, then everyone, dear Consul, will
know that you stole the statue.
So: pay up: half and half: $500,000

f⁰ 7

Salini ponders
what is there in these different stories
      Koala: bizarre tale of double agents
      Magistrate   revenge (retribution)
      The Crypt   revenge
      53   crime of passion

allusions to Serval
      place of birth
      fact that he had a pseudonym
      holiday haunt
      one of his ties
nothing about his activities in the resistance, in politics, business
nothing about his private life   Not much all told
                                          or else everything
                                        is in code

For a while Sahni must speculate
that Serval is not dead
(that like the narrator of *53 Days*
he'll find he's guilty of the crime Serval is planning)

Police: obviously we checked all the names which we found in the
book

    There were indeed a Coulibaly and a Tchicaya and 2 Saunier
    brothers at Collège Geoffroy-Saint-Hilaire at Etampes
    but most of the names seem to have been invented
    the book's author must have been a *pion* or a pupil at Etampes
    at any rate has a fairly precise recall of the town

f° 8

I shall recapitulate briefly:
an American megalomaniac has engaged
 in murky machinations
to lay his hands on a statue of Diocletian unearthed
at the site of Castellum Acridium, near Sakka Pass
in the region of Kolorno.
The French cultural attaché, Mirouet, is taken
to be the American's accomplice
He is recalled to Paris, where he goes to ground
but before disappearing
he speaks at length to Robert Serval
According to what Serval told Lise about that conversation
Mirouet claimed to be the fall guy
of a scam set up
by the Black Hand.
Serval investigates, discovers
the truth and tells it in his own way
in a book called *The Crypt*.
Fearing for his life, he gives the typescript
to the Consul, who then asks me to examine it.
Meanwhile, the Black Hand hauls me in, asserts that it had
nothing to do with the affair and hints
that the Consul may well be mixed up in it.

f° 9

deciphering hieroglyphs in Nan

f° 10

Did Serval need money that much?
Why not: his gambling debts

f⁰ II

Outline *53 Days*

| Hypothesis |

As soon as they find the Cave
the affair seems to become clear
there's a motive: *résistants'* revenge
and a sharpener (the Chartreuse maquis affair) but nothing is
known about any   possible
                              "survivors"
It's not known how   Tempe and Chabert
they managed   search for Tempe
and they can't be   and Chabert
found

| QUESTION |

How does the real murderer know that nobody will go and look in
the cave

Only when they've got the explanation of the 2 murderers
do they reconstitute the affair   NO NEED
so it's a good idea all the same if the "Consul" was a comrade of
    Serval's in the Resistance
So change the story on p. 21 (for instance, they thought they had
the culprit when the enquiry revealed that one of the staff of the
agency organizing the expedition had previously been sacked from
his job as an accountant with FAP for fraud

so when Patricia and "the Consul" decide to eliminate Serval, "the Consul" goes through what happened to him and to Serval in the maquis
to find an affair of treason which might justify such a long-delayed revenge
and he comes across the British commando business

Since "the Consul" and "the prof" claim the murder
they can't deny it when they're questioned before
the body is found.
so mustn't begin to mention the Consul until after the corpse is found.

f⁰ 12

Then the luminous and fearful truth
came to me:
the Consul had understood
that Serval
was blackmailing him
and had responded in the
most efficient way:
by killing him.
Then he cooked up
his comedy so that
by a means I had not yet fathomed
the culprit would end up being me!

217   Bulo: hired killer
     ↓
    Bulow

12   Joseph Boss
      Pepe
      Gold-topped walking stick
      Fall of ministry

f⁰ 13

That's about it. You could also
reckon that ROUARD = MIROUET
especially if you take account of ROUARD's first
name (which is given only once in *The Crypt)* and
MIROUET's, which is André

	REMIROU	ARD
AND	REMIROU	ET

to establish the guilt of anyone at all
on these clues alone
seems to me to be not remotely plausible

---

f⁰ 14

Detailed investigation of the Chartreuse affair
Where?   WW2   history archives
          French   survivors   which?
          English   "   "

after which: the affair reconstituted (Serval traitor)
                                        (melodramatically)
    return to cave: he's there, dead: ~~murder claimed~~ ? ~~by the 2~~
                                       ~~commando survivors~~
                                       yes, but who did it
where does the <u>gun</u> come from?   how
where does the <u>uniform</u> come from? why
                                                      but it is a lead
                                          gun
                                          uniform

the murder of Serval was committed by H and J
H being "the Consul"
J being the teacher (narrator)

Black Ring-file, folio 15: Sketch map of Grianta

fᵒ 16

The Consul pretends (for my benefit)
not to understand the text at all.
In fact he sees right through it
and he <u>kills Serval</u>.

Why did he give me the job of investigating
the book?
Because he'll use
my investigation <u>to pin
Serval's murder on me.</u>

fᵒ 17(1/1)

Schedule				
28 chapters			28 chapters	
280 pages			4 days per chapter	
3 pages per day = 94 days			or 112 davs	
Dec	31		dec	31
J	31	62	J	31
F	28	90	F	28
M	4	4	March	22
typ 8		= 12 March	typ 9	
corr 3		15 March	hand in	on 31 March
			exactly 2.5	ppd

fᵒ 18 (1/2)

Cold city
Hot city
Commando
Chartreuse
Stendhal and Saint-Réal
Patricia Serval
Lise

The Crypt
Magistrate is the murderer
The Koala Case Mystery
"Un r est un m"
"the Consul"
relationship between Crypt and Grianta
relationship *53 Days* and Serval
mirror allusions
Stendhal allusions
The truth   28
narrator in love
narrator's hypotheses
        Salini's hypotheses
police reports, intelligence service reports, publisher's reader's
    report
"the black hand"
Enquiries re Serval-Réal
Enquiries re Serval-Louviers
Enquiries re Tempe
Enquiries re the Consul (*53 Days*)

f⁰ 19 (211)

SCHEDULE
28 chapters   28 chapters
5 days per chapter   4 days per chapter
or 140 days   or 112

December	31		December	31	
January	31	62	January	31	
Feb	28	90	Feb	28	90
March	31	121	March	22	
April	19	140	Typing	8	
Typing	10				

Hand-in on Monday 3 <u>May</u> for publication on 15 JUNE	Hand-in on Wednesday 31 March for launch on 15 May
(roughly) 2 ppd	(roughly) 2.5 ppd

f⁰ 20 (2/2)

aurh
burh murh   for ages the problem seemed to him to be insoluble
curh nurh
durh
furh
gurh

the problem isn't insoluble: all you need
to do is to shift all the clues uttered
by one notch

The blind-eye mirror by X tells the tale
of a man who finds in a novel
a character whose biography matches
his own word for word

X once imagined a story
without a beginning or an end
it's the story of a novelist
on a bus who
meets a man who

f⁰ 21 (2/3)

$13 + 18 = 31$
$25 + 27 = 52$
$37 + 36 = 73$
$49 + 45 = 94$

f⁰ 22 (2/4)

In A

f⁰ 23 (2/5)

53 Days

Grianta the Consul – Serval's disappearance
    Etampes
The narrator reads *The Crypt* = III–IV
Working hypotheses
Questioning of witnesses (the party)
Meets Lise = VII
The "black hand"
Investigation of Serval=Réal

8.   What is encrypted in *The Crypt*
     The Magistrate is the Murderer, The Koala Case
9.   2nd meeting with Lise. Mysterious witnesses?
10. Narrator in love
11. The fearful hypothesis: the Consul killed Serval and fiddled
     everything so I should be guilty
12. The narrator discovers the corpse . . . of the Consul!
13. Epilogue
14. disappearance of Serval. Investigation. Bogged down. Salini
     called in.
15. Salini reads *53 Days* then sees Patricia. Relationship book-
     Serval
16. Where to start? Hot track? Cold track? Etampes (Bordeaux)
17. Return to book: "Un R est un M"? M = mirror
18. Stendhal and St Réal ⟶ the Chartreuse
19. Go over the Resistance affair: the commando, the cave
20. Find the cave again. Serval's body found there.
     Yes but why how
21. Search for the 2 survivors. Tempe and "Chabert"
          Enquiries about them. <u>NOTHING</u>

22. SUM up. Why the book. Return to book
        the "Chabert" trail and the "Consul" trail
23. 2nd meeting with Patricia: hypotheses
24. the cold country
25. the hot country: Chabert trail picked up again
        <u>with the help of the book</u>: THAT'S THE
        CRUCIAL POINT
26. Chabert
27. Chabert's "confession"
28. Epilogue
        the truth the harsh truth
  how it happened
  how it was all dolled up

f⁰ 24 (2/6)

	Clues in The Crypt	What the narrator thinks	The Truth	What the police will think
Motive		the Consul kills Serval who knows he has done a murder	Serval kills Lise's lover, the Consul	the Narrator, in love with Lise, kills her lover the Consul
Material evidence Witness Alibi				

Miroir
Miroir Spirit
Daily Razor
Spiegel
(dans les Reflets
miroir
Ikrough a glass darkly
glace
lunettes
l'Espiègle
MIRO IR
retroviseur
"reflechir"
image
miroir de sorcière
reflets dans un oeil d'or
Sous Georges au Miroir
Palais des Glaces
Ray Bam
Blanche Neige
miroir grossissant
miroir à 3 faces
glace de poche
Psyché

Glace (Sorbet)
jatte à glace
Galerie des glaces
corps miroir

miroir
ad (miroir)
speculer
voir (au joker)
regard (bouche d'égout)
"Morori"
"Rimori"
Tain
le Retour m...
Stade du Miroir
Sonnet de Mallarmé
miettes
point de mire

Mirolier
mirage
mirobolant
mirifique
l'Emir Ovar.chik
MeRe
MaRee
MauRe
MoiRe
MuRe
MaRie
MaRe
MaRi
MouRiR
MuRieR
MeRou
MoReau
MoiRe
MoRue
aven qu Rever
inverser RaMB
RoMec
RaiMu
RiMe
RoMe
RaMi
RaMeau
RaMi
(Sam) REMc
RoMi

Black Ring-file, folio 25: List of allusions to the word "mirror"

f⁰ 26 (3/2)

53 DAYS: CALENDAR										
MAY						JUNE			JULY	
Monday	22	29	6	13	20	27	3	10	17	24	1
Tuesday	23	30	7	14	21	28	4	11	18	25	2
Wednesday	24	1	8	15	22	29	5	12	19	26	3
Thursday	25	2	9	16	23	30	6	13	20		
Friday	26	3	10	17	24	31	7	14	21		
Saturday	27	4	11	18	25	1	8	15	22		
Sunday	28	5	12	19	26	2	9	16	23		

f⁰ 27 (3 /3)

1. On 15 May
2. the Marquis professed
3. (he) soon found
4. Nothing could wake him
5. This whole adventure
6. We shall sincerely grant
7. It is of such insignificant little details
8. And so less than a month after his arrival
9. (. . .) He had great difficulty falling asleep, and his sleep was troubled
10. Whilst lecturing himself at the same time
11. On coming out from the (archbishop's palace) (he) ran to
12. The Jew
13. All the ideas
14. During
15. Two hours later
16. Well,
17. The Count
18. So
19. ambition

20. One night
21. At the time
22. During the day
23. In the midst of this general uproar
24. the duchess held delightful soirées
25. the arrival of
26. the only moments during which
27. This conversation
28. Swept along by events

f° 28 (3/4)

(1, 6) or else 7	13	20		33	53
14	26	40		66	126
40	80	146		146	
				272	

relative weight of each of the 5 novels

Koala	Magistrate	Crypt	53	"53"
2	34	36	70	126

id est

| 1 | 17 | 18 | 35 | 53 Fibonacci |

try to keep to it but no
matter if it overruns. It's
just a detail

(not enough for *Koala*, too much for *Magistrate*, very fair for the
last 3)

f° 29 (3/5)

	Real culprit	Real victim	Mirror victim	Mirror culprit
The M is the M	Vidornaught	Angèle		Fly
CRYPT	Rouard	Vichard	Rouard	Vichard
53D	Serval	Consul	Serval	Narrator
"53D"	Mme Serval	Serval	Serval	"Consul"
	+ Consul	(inheritance)	(Resistance)	(network)
	(lover)			Chabert

f° 30 (3/6)

> (as in *Lolita, The Conversions, Poussière de soleils*, a
> chase along a ready-made trail which is adjusted
> depending on whether or not he finds the flow
> chart)

S, MD, ex-minister, holder of the Resistance medal, is found
murdered, in his car, on Friday
10 July, Place X, in Grenoble
Discreet investigation produces nothing
His car
his attaché case
the Ms *53 Days* – "Un R est un M qui se P le L de la R"
Investigation in Paris
what was he doing in Grenoble?
Salini starts over from the book
the novel describes the false death of Serval
but a Serval is really dead

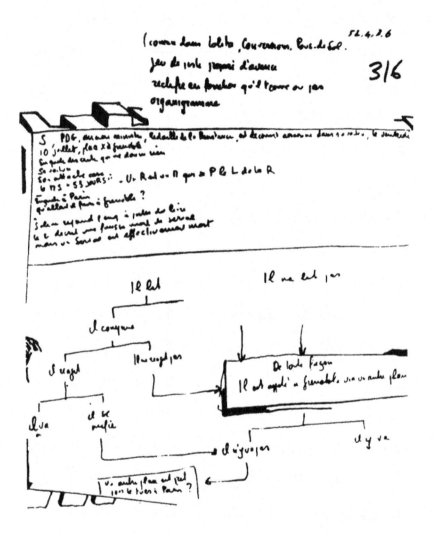

Black Ring-file, folio 30: Shows Perec thinking in shapes

f⁰ 31 (3/7)
typed in
part

"53 Days"	53 Days	The Crypt	Magistrate	The Koala Case Mystery
Paris	Grianta	Gotterdam	Paris?	Newcastle
Patricia Serval née Humphrey	Réal alias Serval	Serval	Angèle	
Serval alias Louviers	The Consul (Vergnaud?)	Vichard	William Vidornaught	Günter Raversi
François-Léon Salini	The narrator	Rémi Rouard	Fly	Frederick Derville
"The Consul" ("Chabert")	Lise	Svendsen (business-man)	Boutin?	Jackson Gillett
"The prof" ("Tempe"?)	Grace Hillof	Derville		Llewlyn P Blanes
"real"	"real becoming fiction in part 2"	fiction	fiction	fiction

f⁰ 32 (3/8)

GENERALITIES

Titles
Stendhal's *incipit*

Plan
Fibonacci

etc.

f° 26 (3/9)
typed

the nine ways in which the number 53 can figure in a Fibonacci
series

1	26	27	53			
3	25	28	53			
5	24	29	53			
7	23	30	53			
9	22	31	53			
1	10	11	21	32	53	
1 6	7	13	20	33	53	
4	15	19	34	53		
1	17	18	35	53		

OoOoOoOoOoOo

SERVAL TELLS THE CONSUL THAT HE KNOWS THE NAR-
RATOR

SERVAL DISAPPEARS

THE CONSUL COMMISSIONS THE NARRATOR TO INVES-
TIGATE SERVAL'S DISAPPEARANCE

THE NARRATOR IS EVENTUALLY CONVINCED THAT
THE CONSUL KILLED SERVAL AND WANTS TO PIN
THE CRIME ON HIM

THE NARRATOR FINDS A CORPSE BUT IT IS NOT SER-
VAL'S. IT IS THE CONSUL'S

SERVAL KILLED THE CONSUL: ALL THE NARRATOR
ACHIEVES IN HIS INVESTIGATION IS TO LAY THE
CLUES WHICH WILL INCRIMINATE HIM (MOTIVES,
WEAPON, OPPORTUNITY, WITNESS, ETC.)

(the narrator may also believe this: that Lise killed Serval; the
Consul, who loves Lise, destroys the clues which would finish
him and replaces them with clues which the narrator thinks he
discovers in his investigation but which serve to incriminate him.

123456789

f° *33*

The narrator finds a corpse but it is the Consul's, not Serval's. Serval killed the Consul: in carrying out his investigation, the Narrator has merely set up the trail which will incriminate him (motive, the weapon of the crime, the opportunity, the witness, etc.)

f° *34 (4/1)*

THIRTEENTH
I suppose that even
the choice of typewriter
was dictated
by the fact that I knew
the supplier well.

f° *35 (4/2)*

> There's no safer place for a fly to land on
> than the fly-trap he might otherwise fly into
>   Lichtenberg

f⁰ 36 (4/2
verso)

the first sentence of this story

the first and last pages of the book were missing

1st part   53 Days   2nd part "Un R est un M qui
se P le L de la R"

f⁰ 37 (4/3)

Thirteenth chapter
I don't know when they decided on a poor provincial teacher as
their fall guy. Probably after the Consul gave me the job of running the French book stand.

They knew the Consul was going to go to France and that it would be easy for Serval to ask him to give me the manuscript.

At first I thought that the events which shook Grianta six weeks ago had got in the way of their plans. But what with the repeated taunts from the entourage of the Interior Minister it wasn't hard to predict that the twenty-fifth anniversary of independence would trigger off riots and bloodshed. On the contrary, it helped them a lot . . .

How did they manage to ensure that I would meet Lise and unwittingly follow the trails, or rather the traps, that she had set for me? What if I had never thought of going to look for that fake typist? I suppose they would have coped in some other way but they must have been sure that I would be hooked by that missing chapter

the final explanation is rather fluffy (the critic specialising in crime fiction notices Patricia explains in chapter 28

f° 38 (4/5)

Thirteenth chapter, end

——————— End of *53 Days* ———————

Yes, of course I'll give this diary to the examining magistrate. But how could I cherish the illusion that it will help me. How can those infinitely malleable things called words ever prove anything other than the useless subtlety of rhetoric?

to rework

Chartre
Tharchesa   CHARTREUSE
Thurchezra   TEURCHEZRA

Black Ring-file, folio 38

f° 39 (s/1)

Fourteenth chapter
Robert Serval's disappearance

Items of the investigation:
    car
    revolver
    attaché case
    53 Days identification of typewriter? And of typing?

Life of Robert Serval

MARKING TIME

53 Days studied by a critic

Eventually, Salini is called in

f° *40 (5/2)*

Meanwhile, Madame Serval, etc.

Salini looks things over

It is a middle-class drawing room, etc.

The disappearance of Robert Serval made a splash in the papers:

Robert Serval, who was decorated for his work in the Resistance and went on to serve as a member of parliament and then as a minister of state, was, as he approached the age of sixty, an exemplary businessman whose energy and dynamism have contributed to making France what she is today.

At any rate, that's what a mass-circulation weekly said

f° *41 (5/3)*

Louviers 4

SEQUENCE "53 D"
The facts of the case
The investigation makes no headway
The investigation makes no headway

> Our only hope, Salini is told, is for that mysterious
> manuscript to contain, in one form or another, the key to our
> problem
> At the moment we still don't know whether Serval is dead or
> alive
> If he is dead, where is the body?

Everything leads us to believe that the document has
something to do with Serval's disappearance
We had it read by a publisher. He said it was pretty superficial
as a "mystery" but quite full of puzzling details nonetheless.
You'll find all that in the files

fº 42 (s/4)

Robert Serval, alias Louviers

Born Rouen, 1918
Education
Hobbies
Travels
Holidays

Joins the Resistance in?   first at Grenoble, where he runs
                                         a bookshop which serves as a
                                         dead-letter box. The letter box
                                         is discovered and he flees to the
                                         mountains of the Chartreuse.

becomes a leader of the maquis
(FFI) in 43 (?) in the Grande
Chartreuse (after the death of
his superior, Captain X, a professional soldier).

The British commando affair?

Involved in street fighting when Grenoble is liberated.
Volunteers: Colmar, etc.
Croix de guerre, médaille de la Résistance, médaille militaire, etc.
Demobbed in 45

Finishes degree in business law?
Goes into politics around 48. Mayor of? Regional councillor.
MP in 59

Widower in 64 (aged 46), remarries a 25-year-old American
in 66
Secretary of State for Foreign Trade in 1972
His time at the ministry turns out to be profitable for the
businesses he deals with
No scandal, but suspicions
Retires from politics in 74
Businesses: textile mills, clothes manufacturing, vegetable
fibres (coconut, raffia, matting fibres, etc.)
Frequent travels to Africa, Middle East, Far East, America.

Divorce pending in 1981. Separated from his wife Patricia née
Humphrey (b. 1941)

f° 43 (6/1)

Fifteenth chapter
Salini:
The so-called Serval finds the solution to the Rouard affair in
a book.
The unfortunate narrator of *53 Days* is supposed to find the
key to the puzzle of Serval's faked disappearance in a book.
So Salini also sought the cause of Serval's quite genuine death
in a book.

f° 44 (6/2)
typed

The author of *53 Days* lays many false trails. For instance,
Robert Serval is the model not only for the character of Robert
Serval, but for the Consul and the narrator too. Like the Consul, Serval was born at Rouen without being of Norman ascent;
like the narrator he had spent several holidays at Veulle-les-Roses.
There were too many details of this kind for them all to be coincidental. Even very minor characters with no direct relevance to
the detective plot had been given some of Robert Serval's traits

– for instance, the club tie with which Grace Hillof was strangled was his (nothing to do with the entirely fictional Blackbells
Military Academy of Arizona: the purely decorative crest was that
of the Florida Spinners' Guild, which had made Serval "Honorary
Spindle" during the French-American Trade Week at Miami,
thought up and promoted by Serval).

Fifteenth chapter

f⁰ 45 (7/1)

Sixteenth chapter

in "53 D" how does Salini interpret Etampes?	HE MUST make something of it
Does he investigate	(make it mean something quite different)

or does he decide that Etampes
= Bordeaux (for instance)
where Serval did his degree?

f⁰ 46 (8/1)

Seventeenth chapter
   So it is in *53 Days* and nothing else that Salini has a chance of
finding something that will get the case off the ground

"Un R est un M qui se P le L de la R"

f⁰ 47 (8/2)

"Un R est un M qui se Pl e L del a R." He keeps coming back to this
cryptic code. He's tried working it out, pages and pages of workings-out. He gives the problem to everyone he bumps into

[The next pages in the black ring-file contain re-expansions (some are by Perec, some by others) of the sentence formula derived from a version of Stendhal's definition of the novel, "Un roman est un miroir qui se promène le long de la route": "Un R est un M qui se P le L de la R." *The procedure could be simulated in English by:*

> A Novel is a Mirror that you Hold to Life
> "A N is a M that you H to L"

which would permit re-expansions such as:
"A noggin is a mug that you hold to lip"
"A name is a moniker that you hesitate to lengthen"
"A neurosis a maladjustment that you heighten to lyricism"
"A novelist is a manipulator that you have to lampoon" and so on.

Amongst the many developed and half developed expansions in Perec's own hand are:

> "Un roman est un miracle qui se prophétise le leitmotiv de la résonance"

> *(A novel is a miracle foretelling for itself the theme of resonance)*

> "Un romancier est un maniaque qui se propose le lemme de la réalite"

> *(A novelist is a maniac who sets himself the lemma of reality)]*

f⁰ 57 (8/11)

"Un R est un M"
obtained many correct versions

"un roi est un monarque"	("a king is a monarch")
"un rat est un mammifère"	("a rat is a mammal")
"un raté est un médiocre"	("a failure is a mediocrity")

"le L de la R"
was much more difficult

and the reflexive verb especially
made most sentences impossible

segments such as
            "Un roturier est un monarque qui se plante"
            ("a commoner is a monarch who muffed it")
hit a dead end straight away

Salini tried practically every verb in the French language
expressions of time   *le lundi de la rentrée* ("On the first
                        Monday of term")
                    le lendemain de la rentrée ("On the
                        second day of term")
        of place   *le long de la rue* ("Along the street")
                    le lieu de la révolte ("The place of the
                        uprising")
                    le luxe de la révolte ("The luxury of
                        revolt")

*f° 58 (8/11
verso)*

RATE $12\,^{34}_{43}$

RAET $13\,^{24}_{42}$

RTAE $14\,^{23}_{32}$

RTEA
RETA   21
REAT   23
                    24

A TE
  ET
R T
  E
  E
A R
  T
  A
T E   31
  R
  R
E A   32
  T   34
$4 \times 3 \times 2$

$$41 \begin{matrix} 23 \\ 32 \end{matrix}$$

$$42 \begin{matrix} 13 \\ 31 \end{matrix}$$

$$43 \begin{matrix} 12 \\ 21 \end{matrix}$$

fº 59 (8/12)

Cl.53J 59 (8/12)

| 14 francs per vol. |

For example the sentence
    "He should never have gone skiing: his left knee's so fragile . . .
you know he has broken it twice already . . ."
could be represented by
  "Un Récidiviste est un Maladroit qui se Pète le Ligament de la
Rotule"
("A recidivist is a clumsy person who buggers the ligament in his
patella") *[. . .]*

f⁰ 60 (8/12
verso)

Investigations
Salini's biography   Enquiries with publishers show
Salini called in   that the book was never
                                    submitted for publication
                                    Looked at by a reader
2. Salini   "Reading note"
                                    (*mise en abyme* of the book)
3. Search for the hot city   Chabert is let's say
False trail   20 in '40
                                    60 in '80

4. False trail 2 (the cold city)

5. The sentence
    Theme of the mirror
    Stendhal etc.

6. Investigation resumed   Find not too quickly
    Serval during the resistance

thereafter a study of the book provides the necessary clues (with
mistakes)
        the Consul ⟶ Stendhal ⟶ Civitavecchia
                   ⟶ Malcolm Lowry
                   ⟶ Duras
        manages in the end to identify one of the
        "survivors"

ƒº 64 (9/1)
typed

Eighteenth chapter

As for the allusions which led to Stendhal, there were so many that
Salini gave up listing them all. In *53 Days,* Robert Serval had a
<u>red</u> Jaguar, in life he had a <u>black</u> one. At the Hilton, the Consul
chose to eat a veal cutlet with spinach as if by chance, but it was of
course Stendhal's favourite dish. Cularo is the name of the village
which became Grenoble centuries later; Grianta is the name of
the castle on the shore of Lake Como where Fabrice del Dongo
spent his childhood, etc.

XXXXXXXXXXXXXX

In *The Magistrate is the Murderer,* Angèle (Angelina) is found
dead in her flat in Rue Saint-Séverin (Sanseverina), whilst the
four deaths in *The Koala Case Mystery* occur in a house in Nasturtium Street, a translation of Rue des Capucines, where Stendhal
was struck down by apoplexy. One of Stendhal's addresses, <u>8 Rue
de Caumartin</u> (where he wrote *La Chartreuse de Parme,* in fact),
is given as that of the narrator of *53 Days* during his student years
in Paris; as for Serval's real address, 71 Rue Murillo, in the Parc
Monceau district, it appears in *The Crypt,* curiously transmogrified into 71 Calle del Moreau, in Muncillo.

@@@@@@@@@@@@

All that would have been so as to make plausible the hype of discovering
the thread in the form of some document from a dying man touched by
repentance Raymond Roussel, *Dust of Suns,* 1, 5.
And here he is on the job, marking out in reverse all the staging
posts towards which our own deduction shave successively led us.
(Same source)

f⁰ 65 (9/2)

Salini reads *53 Days*,
and ends up finding Stendhal.
But what Stendhal?
The epigraph: snow,
Saint-Réal: Chambéry.
Speculation on reality and mirrors.
Allusions to *La Chartreuse*.
THEREFORE led back to the Chartreuse maquis

f⁰ 66 (9/3)

St Réal
Dom Carlos
Nouvelle historique
This story is drawn from Spanish, French, Italian and Flemish
authors who have written about the period in which it is set. The
principal amongst them are M de Thou, Aubigné, Brantôme,
Cabrera, Adriana, Natalis Comes, Dupleix, Mathieu, Mayerne,
Mézeray, Le Laboureur sur Castelnau, Strada, Meteren, the his-
torian of Don Juan of Austria, the eulogies of Father Hilarion da
Costa, a Spanish book on the words and deeds of Philip II, an
account of the death and burial of his son, etc. It is also drawn
from manuscript and printed sources pertaining to the story, including a little book in verse entitled *Diogenes*, which deals with
it exhaustively, and a manuscript by M de Peiresc directly on the
same subject.

cf. on Don Carlos, Stendhal, *Journal*, 24 July 1804

*f⁰ 67 (9/3
verso)*

Discourse III " . . . like mirrors . . . "

Preface to *Life of Octavie*: "the happy genius of an author who leads
you as in a game along the most delightful
paths"
DuBellay   "Ou, comme en un miroir, l'homme sage contemple
Tout ce qui est en lui, ou de laid ou de beau"
("Where, as in a mirror, the wise man looks upon/All
that is in him, be it ugly or beautiful")
Speculum: mirror (of doctrine)
Don Quixote "a mirror of knight errantry"
Shakespeare   *Hamlet III*   the actor's craft   "the mirror up to
nature"
Fielding   Pléiade 1964, p. 187

Sanréal is the name of a character in Lucien Leuwen (chapters V
and CX)
There are 171 pseudonyms used by Stendhal

SHETLAND
STENDHAL

S INTREAL
  ↓ ↓
  H D

(Henri) (Dominique
  SHTNDEAL
  STENDHAL

f° 68 (9/4)

MONTELLO
In the preface to *Armance*
    "the author follows another path"
    "they showed a mirror to the audience: is it their fault if ugly
    people passed in front of the mirror?
    What side is a mirror on?"
In *The Red and the Black*, ch. XXII (3rd appearance)
    in the § where there is "a pistol-shot in the midst of a concert"
    . . . and your book is no longer a mirror
August 1838, preface to *Lucien Leuwen*
the mirror image is in Marivaux, Proust (etc.)
many of the epigraphs are invented (according to Martineau, *Le
Coeur de Stendhal*, vol II, p. 155)

Saint-Réal, Discourse IV "making them see in history, as in a mirror, the depiction of their faults"

*f° 69 (9/34
verso)*

In the *Conspiracy of the Spaniards against Venice*, two of the
conspirators are called Robert et Laurent Brulard
"we could go a long way"
and
"as in a mirror"
are found in the 7 discourses on the uses of history
The Author deduces that Saint Réal thought that "history is a
mirror," etc. and that Stendhal replaced history by novel.
Yeah?

f⁰ 70 (9/5)

Bassette
The Red and the Black, chapter XIII A novel: 'tis a mirror taken along a road
R&B XIX "Well! sir, a novel is a mirror taken along a highway"

1836 preface to *Lucien Leuwen*   A novel is a mirror
never located in Saint-Réal

Allusions to Saint-Réal
    letter to Pauline   6 XII 1801
                       22 I 1803
                       June 1804
                       August 1804

Editions of Saint Réal complete works
Amsterdam   1730, 1749
Paris   1712, 1745, 1755, 1757
Selected works   2 vols 1804

Find out about OTWAY *Venice preserved*   (Stendhal,
(subject comes from Conspiracy against Venice) *Courrier anglais*, article on X de Maistre)

f⁰ 71 (9/5 verso)

BASSETTE, Louis. "Sur une épigraphe du Rouge et Nair de Stendhal et Saint-Réal," *Stendhal-Club* 35 (15 April 1967) 2411–253. 4° Z 5509
MONTELLO, J *Un maître oublié de Stendhal. Saint-Réal*. Paris, Seghers, 1970. 156 pp. 4° Z 6734

f° 72 (9/6
verso)   CULARO

Eighteenth chapter

I received a letter from the minister of the interior
    announcing that I was to
      go to CULARO with the Consul Saint-Vallier
          Stendhal, *Oeuvres intimes*, p. 1287

f° 73 (9/7)

Eighteenth
chapter

It is known that Saint-Réal never wrote that sentence
which appears twice in Stendhal's *The Red and the Black* in slightly
different forms
In Saint-Réal's mind it was not a matter
of the <u>novel</u> but of <u>History</u>

Did it mean that the "novel" (*53 Days*)
referred to a real historical fact
was its reflection
(a little like R&B being the very distant
transcription of the trial of Z?)

The Red and the Black must appear

Saint-Réal in Stendhal's life
    la SAINTE REALITE ("sacred reality")

Madrid (REAL Madrid)

appeal to an ever absent reality

The Red: the reds
   the red hand
The Black?

It was in V's will that proof was found
[...]
"the harsh truth" → Danton
   R&B
so a "Dantonesque" character
   cf. Could he be a Danton (Mathilde, about Julien)

f° 73 (9/7
verso)

DYLAN THOMAS
Vision and Prayer
12 poems in 2 parts of 6 each
the first 6 as diamonds
   from 1 to 9 feet then → 1 foot
the other 6 nested
syllabic coupling

f° 74 (9/8)

Eighteenth chapter
the manuscript is given to a Stendhal specialist
he picks up all the allusions
so just for the first 3 chapters
   Chalier, the name of the manager of the El Ghazâl Hôtel, is one
of Henri Beyle's pseudonyms, for the *History of Painting in Italy*
   Alzire, the name of the street where Serval's Jag is found, comes
from an unfinished story, based on Scarron, of which HB wrote 75 p.
on 10 October 1838.

fº 75 (10/1)

In a diary belonging to
Bordinet head of the
paramilitary police at
the following note is found
Louviers   Manufacture of forged papers

fº 76 (10/2)

Nineteenth chapter

The whole career of Serval, alias Louviers,
in the Resistance is reconstituted
(the pseudonym is not the hero)
    – Joins Resistance
    – Dead-letter box
    – Forged papers
    – Avoids STO
    – Helps the British
    – The Chartreuse
    – The COMMANDO
    – The affair of the cave at . . .
      his sorties
      the survivors
    – The Hardy affair?
    – insurmountable difficulties of reconstruction.

fº 77 (10/3)

Nineteenth chapter

Serval's codename was Louviers.
At a banquet held by former members of the Resistance,
which Serval had been asked to chair when he was

still undersecretary of state,
he explained how he had chosen
his pseudonym. He thought first of
Rouen, because that was where he was born.
But his CO explained that he would be
taking an unnecessary risk. The Gestapo and the
Paramilitary Police employed specialists to decode
pseudonyms. Some of them were really quite bright.
One was even said to have found
the real name of one of the leaders of
the maquis in the Creuse from two *noms de guerre*
    which he had used in succession,
        having been obliged to drop the first one after

f° 78 (10/3
verso)

his liaison agents had been caught. First he was
called *Persée* ("Perseus"), and then *Fleury* ("Flowery").
What is the real name of a chap who
takes the name *Persée* and then *Fleury*?
The specialist got it in one: *Panier,* and he was right: the guy really
was called Pannier.
    In fact, Salini notes, Louviers is but
        the consonantal palindrome of SERVL
                S$_e$RV$_a$L – LouVieRS

Black Ring-file, folios 79/80: List of stations on the Sydney–Wollongong
line, and names of the commando

fᵒ 79 (10/4)

List of
the commando
dropped into
the Chartreuse
(Operation "   ")

hidden by Serval
in the . . . cave
in the Chartreuse,
then,
in the cave,
all arrested

An internal landing
was planned
(Vercors, Massif central,
Chartreuse)
and this drop was
an advance party

Hurstvaal
Hurstville

fᵒ 81(10/5)

What Serval Louviers really did in the Resistance.
A – runs bookshop–letter box
B – flees to the Chartreuse
C – takes the British commando to the cave

D –takes part in the fighting for the liberation of Grenoble
E – goes to fight in Alsace

AND THAT'S ALL

Patricia: There was nothing heroic about Serval, nor was he remotely like a traitor. Wouldn't have known how. Swept along by events

Two days later, the commando is handed over to another group of the maquis, and they are ambushed. All killed on the spot except Sébastien Tempe (a Frenchman in the OSS) and   alias Chabert, the leader of the other group. After interrogation and torture, Tempe is imprisoned at   , whence he manages to escape.   alias Chabert vanishes

After the war, there is an enquiry based on Tempe's account. Louviers's name is mentioned, favourably for the most part. A search is made for Chabert. But in vain. (Let's suppose Chabert is dead.) When "the Consul" and Patricia decide on their coup, they agree that "the Consul" will play the role of a "Chabert" who has proof of Louviers's guilt, finds Tempe, and murders Louviers. So far so good. But what does Tempe say?

f° 82 (*10/6*)

19th
I propose to take you to that cave in the forest of   to find the corpse of Robert Serval.

f⁰ 83 (10/7)

The British commando (OSS?) consisted of

	5 Englishmen, Sutherland,
Hidden in a building	Oatley, Mondale, Penshurst,
at the Chartreuse monastery	Sydenham
for 48 hours	3 Canadians, Redfern, Rockdale,
then taken to a	Hurstville
cave	1 New Zealander, Kogarah
	2 Frenchmen, Tempe, Como
	1 Lebanese, Jannali

And then?
A   The paramilitaries surrounding the cave
slaughtered everyone
except the commando's CO
and Serval alias Bérot,
who were handed over to the Gestapo

Post-war investigation
Who betrayed them?
(if they were betrayed)
Bérot, who escaped and was later decorated?
Sutherland?
PROBLEM; the instigators
of *53 Days* must be French
Let's say Tempe and Como
are French (Free French)
          Forêt des Meuniers *[?]* Gorges de Malessard

f° 84 (10/8)

19th chapter

At the heart of this story is a disturbing episode which perhaps forms the cornerstone of the whole affair	1942 4 Sept: STO introduced

43
30 Jan Paramilitaries
16 Feb STO
April: United Resistance Movement
Combat + FTP* + *Libération*
15 May CNR**
21 June Jean Moulin arrives
11 Nov Resistance demo parades at Oyonnax
20 Jan 44   Court martial of *résistant*
Les Glières

Gathering of *résistants* end 43
parachute reception team
set up on 30 1 44: 120 men
incl. officers and NCOs
from the 27th Alpine Light
Infantry from Annecy who are
part of the armistice army
dissolved in Nov 42 CO Morel
alias Tom, 2nd in command
    Aujol alias Bayard
Joined by STO deserters
FTP, Spanish republicans
500 men in all
paramilitaries assault
attack the maquis near
Entremont

43
July   etc.
landings in Italy

1 Feb Operations against the maquis in the Savoie
25 March   Les Glières
6 June   Overlord landing
10 June   Oradour
13–21   Vercors massacre

15 August landings in Provence
23 Liberation of Grenoble
4 Oct   Tribunal against collaborators

*FTP: *Francs-tireurs partisans,* partisan guerrilla.
**CNR: *Conseil national de la résistance,* National Resistance Council

(Flying Squad) on 13 Feb 44
attack by 12,000 Wehrmacht
soldiers
    air force
    then infantry on 22 March
    taken on 25   45   2 Feb Colmar taken

f° 85 (10/9)

Nineteenth chapter

This is what Salini said to Inspector H:
It is now clear to me that the disappearance and in all probability
the murder of Serval are connected with what happened a few weeks
before the liberation of Grenoble (Sept. 44?) in the mountain of La
Grande Chartreuse, between Grenoble and Chambéry. That is what
the book clearly hints at, it offers no other lead

    The Intelligence Service file on Serval is not a thick one. It
shows that Serval joined the Resistance in Lyon in 1942; one of
his old school chums was part of an intelligence network which
looked after airmen who had baled out over France and helped to
get them back to Britain. He asked Serval to run a little bookshop
used by the network as a letter box. A few weeks later the letter
box was blown.

f° 86
(10/11 –
10/12)

                  19th
           The Hardy affair
At Delestraint's request, Hardy, head of Rail-Sabotage,
prepares a general sabotage plan with an engineer called Heilbronn

Delestraint (Vidal) wants to meet Hardy (Didot) on 9 June at
Muette metro station
     Gives task to his assistant AUBRY   Letter box in Rue
  Bouteille
Aubry passes the job on to his secretary Madame Raisin
Madame Raisin leaves the message (not in code)

Multon (Lunel) gets knowledge of the message
(not known if he put it back in the box. Hardy
claims he never knew about the rendez-vous)

but Hardy has a different rendezvous in Paris on sabotage business
His fiancée Mlle Bastien got him his ticket

on the train he travels with a Vichy official: Cressol
Multon and Moog are in the next compartment (going to Paris to
    arrest Delestraint)

Hardy recognises Lunel (Multon) and tips off "another" *résistant*
Lunel recognises Hardy whom he knows as "Carbon"
At Chalon the German police, tipped off by Lunel, arrest Hardy
    (and Cressol)
and Barbie comes to get him almost immediately

Meanwhile Lunel and Moog pick up Delestraint at Muette metro
    station
Delestraint suspects nothing and goes on to Pompe metro station
to collect 2 other colleagues

10 June   Nonetheless   Barbie   releases   Hardy   after
   six   hours   questioning (pp. 143–4)

12 June
2 days later Heilbronn is arrested after a meeting with Hardy
The Gestapo tortures him and wants him to confess that he is
Didot!

Meanwhile after Delestraint's arrest
Jean Moulin summons several people to Lyon
to reorganise the Secret Army
Lassagne, inspector of the SA south zone and born in Lyon is
entrusted with setting up the meeting
Amongst those called, Aubry, opposed to Moulin's plans, decides to
go there with Hardy to press his case (147)
the Aubry-Hardy interview is witnessed by Barbie!! (148)

On the evening of Sunday, 20 June 1943, 5 men know the rendez-
vous point: Moulin, Lassagne, Lacaze, Larat (liaison agent) and
Dr Dugougon (who is lending his villa)
4 others have intermediate pick-ups
Aubrac, Schwartzfeld whom Moulin will bring himself
Aubry (to rendezvous with Lassagne)
Hardy (brought along by Aubry)

f° 87
(10/11)

Lassagne, Aubry and Hardy arrive

Mlle Deletraz (a double agent) has followed Hardy
she tells Barbie
but takes steps so that the Gestapo
won't reach the place before 2:45
(the meeting was at 2)
But Moulin Aubry and Schwarzfeld
are also 45 minutes late!!!

Arrest!
The Gestapo knows that Max (Jean Moulin) is
one of those arrested
but do not know which

Hardy manages to escape!
arrested by French police
who hand him over to the Gestapo
escapes again

f° 88
(10/14 –
10/15)

3rd appearance:
Pléiade p. 576
2nd P p. 557

Or else
the man who calls himself R. Serval
and passes for a former hero of the Resistance, code-name ~~Bérot~~
Louviers, is in reality Barbinet,head of the paramilitary police at?
(who arrested, tortured and killed RS and took his place on x x
1944.)
Or else   he <u>went over</u> after arrest by the Gestapo and is in
               fact responsible for the capture of the entire
               maquis group.
In case 1: 2 former maquis of RS's group recognise him
In case 2: 2 survivors of RS's group (the "Consul" and X) obtain
proof of his treachery and execute him

History of the maquis
R&B p. 698: Julien Sorel
buried in a cave
above Verrières

the isle (arms cache)
the Chartreuse
the cave

The Germans come twice
to inspect the Chartreuse

Forging ID papers
Sabotage
Parachute drops

f° 89 (12/1)

1943
Le Colonel Chabert
by René le Henaff
with Raimu
and Marie Bell

f° 90 (13/1)
typed

Twenty-second chapter
Salini deciphers the enigma of "Un R est un M qui se P le L de la R," and draws from it these conclusions: if there is a hidden message in the book, then it is probably something like: "things are not what they seem (or seemed) to be." In *The Crypt*, the detective narrator Serval investigates the death of Rouard to discover that the murderer is Vichard; but the aforementioned Rouard is not dead at all; his faked death is the tool of a perfect crime whose victim would have been Vichard if Serval had not uncovered the "real truth." In *53 Days*, the anonymous narrator believes the Consul has killed Serval, and is trying to get him to carry the can; whereas the truth is the opposite – Serval, with the assistance of Lise, has killed the Consul and has set things up so that the narrator-detective is inexorably incriminated. "Reality" is thus the opposite of what you first think, and the problem is to choose one of them any possible opposites. It's quite possible that Serval isn't dead; it's quite possible that he is dead, but that the murderer is not X as we are led to believe, but Y; it's quite possible that Serval has taken his own life and wants to pin his death on X, or on Y . . .

The narrator of *53 Days* says, à propos of *The Crypt*: "In Serval's novels, as with Ellery Queen and others, the author's pseudonm is the same as the name of his hero." If we take this sentence as a clue to Serval's disappearance, how should we read it? In the novels of Ellery Queen, and this can be checked easily, the hero's name and the *nom-de-plume* are indeed identical. In his "real" life, Serval-*nom-de-guerre*, that is to say Serval alias Bérot in the Resistance, was also a hero. Is that what is wrong? Is that what the unknown author of *53 Days* is trying to tell us? — That the *nom-de-plume* is NOT the hero; Serval alias Bérot is NOT a hero: HE IS A TRAITOR.

ms.

Or even: Ellery Queen are two men, but Serval is one means "Serval is two," there are two Servals, the true and the false

****

typed

There is something nightmarish about all of this. Salini finds himself in the same position as the narrator of *53 Days*, and at times the namelessness of that narrator plunges him into a curious state of anxiety, to the point where he almost wonders if he hasn't been explicitly designated by the author to conduct this most unusual investigation. The idea is patently absurd. Before being asked to take the case on, he knew neither Serval nor his wife, but he can't help identifying with the amateur detective who is so easily led astray. Sometimes he feels the need to reassure himself by going through all the features which distinguish him from the narrator-character – he's twenty years older, he's never been a French teacher in the capital city of a tropical dictatorship,he plays neither bridge nor tennis. But he does have a liking for detective stories and for crosswords . . .

and then above all else there's this way of twisting and turning apparently ordinary pieces of information so as to squeeze a hidden meaning out of them, this endless, pernickety explication de texte which purports to pierce the story's obscurity but which in fact only sets its wheels in motion . . .What exactly is he supposed to be doing? How can he be sure of finding any bearings in a gallery of distorting mirrors?

# # # # # # # # #

It's all the rein the opening lines: the city under military patrol, the state of emergency: of course, it's just the lamentably ordinary picture of a police state – but it's also France under the Occupation, with the Flying Squad, the "Resistance" (of café waiters) and even a curious allusion to the "patriotic choice" of "good French [wines] and true." There aren't any words which would give too much away too soon, such as "maquis," but could "Hermitage" not be decoded into *"La Chartreuse"*?

P P P P P P

f⁰ 91 (14/1)

TWENTY-THIRD CHAPTER
In the middle of the month of January, Salini
contacts Patricia again. She
can see him at her home in Rue Murillo.
He asks her:
        "Did he talk to you about this man Chabert?"
        "Not that I can recall."
        "He told you what he did in the war?"

"Of course . . . but rather vaguely . . . spoke of the Chartreuse
. . . nothing very detailed"
    Salini sighs.
    "It's our only lead . . .   no one knows what he's called."
Salini goes home.
He looks up his copy of Balzac's *Le Colonel Chabert*
reads
Chabert had two friends, two old
comrades-in-arms,
one called BOUTIN
    who lives with two performing polar bears;
and an "Egyptian" (a veteran of the Egyptian Campaign)
called Louis Vergnaud.
They're the only ones who recognise and help him,
alongside the solicitor Derville (later on).
    NOW these three names plus some details appear in

f⁰ 92 (15/1)

                                    24/25
    How to find Chabert
    Salini rereads Balzac
    Comes across Derville
                    X
            and   Y
        thus Chabert
Hypotheses about the origin
of the pseudonym   Panier → Persée
                              ↘ Fleury

Serval-Rouen-Louviers
SRVL   LVRS

so Chabert
the film came out in December 43
when "Chabert" joined up

there were many Chaberts in the Resistance, particularly after the release of René le Henaff's film. Chabert is the one who says "I" in the book – the narrator. His name, Veyraud, is mentioned once only.

Veyraud . . . but there is no character called Veyraud in Balzac's story

true, but there are many, including the <u>former</u> Comtesse Chabert,
who are called <u>Ferraud</u>
"se non è vero . . ."

f° 93 (16/1)

Twenty-fifth Chapter
the hot city

f° 94 (16/2)

Salini begins by getting it quite wrong
he looks for the town described
(the hot one)
ends up in a Hilton at Bahrein (Qatar, Abu Dhabi?)
then the cold city
(Copenhagen, soon?)
or Montreal from memory + next February?

My trip to Australia will have taken exactly 53 days!
(with a margin of 9 hours: departed on 27 [August] at midnight, return on 19 [October] at 9) + 9 hours time-zone change (cancelled out)

On 15 May, for the 20th anniversary of independence (55–75)	Minimum temperature at night 30° day 37–41°
There was a pianist of implausible nationality who was	the sky's not blue it is white

playing much the same thing as
S could have heard at the
Closerie des Lilas
He ate   cooking done by a Dutch chef
He did not see the town
He didn't really want to see it as
if he knew already that he   This medley of shacks and
would see nothing   squares (and above all the
                                      furnace-like
He combed the telephone   heat preventing a European
directories   from
He watched television   moving before 6.00 p.m. when
                                      the
                                      shops shut)

> The typescript
>   identification of the typewriter: Underwood 4 000000
>   paper
>   typed by an amateur (all the letters have equal weight
>   therefore typed with 2 or 4 fingers CHECK THIS: odd)
>   way of checking: when you photocopy, it gets paler and
>   paler, but the letters typed with the little finger go pale faster

Real Arabs in their white robes—
and their red check turbans held in place
by sausage-like things

Saw a wedding from the distance in the Gilgamesh reception
room: costume was a fabulous mixture of traditional and rather
ghastly European. TV taking closeup of the bouquet

f° 96 (17/1)

When we began
to work out how
we might tackle

the murder of Serval, I was
reading *La Chartreuse de Parme*. You know how
things are. When something is on
your mind, you find it cropping up everywhere.
As soon as you're hungry you notice
restaurants all the time, or if you're under treatment
you notice that there's a chemist's every fifteen yards. In a word

f° 97(17/1
verso)

I began to see
coincidences on
almost every page
first of all the Chartreuse
then the fact that Fabrice
needed forged documents
to get to the battle of Waterloo when
Serval actually
forged papers himself
and so on

f° 98(17/2)

Patricia (about the Author): I think he even used personal memories
            . . . that didn't bother me, no more than the fact that
            there are false trails . . .as long as all the details I asked
            for are present in the text

            details, allusions, and even plays on words but that
            doesn't bother

f° 99 (17/3)

Twenty-eighth chapter

We met Perec at Zagora, in
the southern part of Morocco.
One day we went on an outing
into the desert with him. Not
by camel, obviously enough,
nor even in a Landrover, but
in an air-conditioned Cadillac.
When we drove past that sign,
                          etc.

Coincidence?

Black Ring-file, folio 99:
First appearance of Perec
as a fictional character

f° 100
(17/4)

Has he made any headway?
There are hundreds or maybe thousands of Boutins and Vergnauds
in the world.
    The idea: a Vergnaud or a Boutin took Chabert as a pseudonym
    because of Balzac (and maybe the film which came out in?)
Colonel Chabert comes back 10 years after and finds his wife married
to Ferraud

"Chabert" with the help of his mistress kills Serval
The truth is once again the opposite (END)

f° 101
(17/5)

THE END:

Salini (to Patricia): Who wrote the book
P: A novelist whom we met at   . he is called GP
       apparently he adores these sorts of problems. We gave him a
       number of key words, themes, names. It was up to him what he
       did with them.
S: You weren't disappointed with the result
P: I haven't really read the book, just checked that all the
       allusions were there. It did not displease me that false trails
       were laid.
S: But why the title, *53 Days*?
P: It's the time Stendhal took to write *La Chartreuse de Parme*.
       You didn't know? We talked about that a great deal when we
       first met. He too wanted to write a book in 53 days. That was
       actually what gave us the idea of the challenge: to take 53 days
       to write a novel for which we would supply this and that piece.
    In fact, he took a lot longer. We had made allowances for
overruns, but in the end
we really had to breathe down his neck . . .

Paris Brisbane Bressuire
1981–1982

f⁰ 102
(17/6)

It was that name Chabert which prompted us to use a book as
the key to the whole affair . . . Colonel Chabert, who comes
back from the dead forty years on . . . But that would have given
a direct lead too early on. It was better to find something else – a
better-known novel. The Chartreuse made us think of Stendhal,
and that's how it all started (Patricia: final explanation)

    We hunted through *La Chartreuse de Parme* and other works by Stend-
hal for elements which could (after a while) be seen as a trail. St Réal,
etc.

        then we looked for a writer

f° 103
(17/7)

Twenty-eighth chapter

The truth (the "harsh truth," as Stendhal or Danton would have said) is given explicitly in this mysterious manuscript: just as Serval, abetted by his lover Lise, murders the Consul and guarantees his own impunity, so "The Consul," abetted by his lover Patricia, murders Robert Serval. But this truth is displayed only to make it impossible to see. Its laughable obviousness is swallowed up by the cloak of fiction.

OTHER NOTES

1. Loose sheets folded into the black ring-file

f⁰ 1

    "53 Days"   takes place   in Paris
the only possible lead is a manuscript entitled
     53 Days   in Grianta
X is asked to find clues about "the disappearance of Robert Serval"
in his unfinished detective novel called
     The Crypt   at Gotterdam   Vichard
                                            (St Réal)

The Magistrate is the Murderer   at
The Koala Case Mystery   at (Australia)

                                            Fly, William
                                          Vidornaught
                                              ↓
                                          the fly
                                          (Lichtenberg)
                                              ↓
                                          Mosca

f⁰ 2

Consul	2nd story	3rd story	1st story
Serval	Detective	Culprit	Victim
~~Xavier~~	Culprit ↑	Victim	Detective
	▼Victim	Detective	Culprit

	53 Days	"53 Days"	*The Crypt*
in the 1st			as narrator
Consul			("author")
Serval			who says I
Xavier			(thus Serval)

	53 Days	"53 Days"	
in the 3rd			
Consul		Culprit	
Serval		Victim	
Xavier		detective	

in the 2nd
the Consul is the victim
Serval is the culprit
Xavier is the detective

01	2	3
Serval	Culprit	Victim
Consul	Victim	Culprit
X (teacher)	Detective	
Y		Detective

f 3

Completely flat style with bravura passages
role of constraints (Oulipian masterpiece)?? in
which case 28 constraints (1 per chapter)
– *Belle absente*
– *Beau présent?*
– lipogram
– palindrome
– pangram
– vowel series
– vowel-consonant-v-c
– the prisoner's constraint
– Delmas's constraint
– snowball

– tautogram
– Mathews's algorithm   3 suspects 3 clues 3 motives <u>or rather</u>
– Graeco-Latin bi-square of 3
– X takes Y for Z

The Crypt
53 D
"53 D"

mystery

	1	2	3
x	A_a	C_c	B_b
y	C_b	B_a	A_c
z	B_c	A_b	C_a

A: detective
B: victim
C: culprit

The Koala Case
        in the 1st book X: Consul is the detective
                        Y: Serval the victim
                        Z: Xavier the culprit

        in the 2nd   Consul is the victim
                        Serval the culprit
                        Xavier the detective

        in the 3rd   Consul is the culprit
                        Serval is the detective
                        Xavier is the victim

f° 4

Members of the Grenoble paramilitaries: Barbier (25 yrs)
Members of the Voiron paramilitaries
X   name presumed to be genuine
(A) Serval, *nom de guerre* Béraud Bérot
        betrayed by ?
        "turned around" by the Gestapo
        group of *n* STO deserters form a maquis
        at X
        in the Chartreuse massif

f⁰ s

Dust of Suns
↓
skull of Ambrosi
↓
the word "sepia"
↓
Pterodactyl Stone
↓
Cournaleux
↓
swallow and martinet
↓
L'Astrée → Valdemont
↓
d'Urfé's letter
↓
albino shepherdess
(Ignacette)
sunshower
↓
Rovilius
↓
humour zones of the preaching knoll on Avenella Island (Flurian)
↓
Varlet's cartoon
↓
golden lily of the purple Turzilo-Selirdian flag
↓
the Okleat stamp
↓
three stars on a cross
↓
the sum of the donation
↓

cube of 5
↓
cube game
↓
rosette
↓
portrait of Antonine Rogissart in a "rosette frame"
↓
L(ibertarian) P(rinciples)
↓
L(ouis) P(hilippe)
↓
Frénu's Café
↓
"Myth through the Ages"
↓
strawberry
↓
Achille Magès's strawberry
↓
the shaft

f⁰ 6

clues in *53 Days*	False leads	What is believed about Serval in the Resistance	What is "true" about Serval in the Resistance
the hot country	Qatar		
the cold country	Reykjavik?		
school friends	Etampes		

business relations?
"Un R est un M" → Chartreuse
                1st "true" lead
The crypt   the cave
The mirror   reversal [?]
                 Stendhal Grenoble ⎫   route from
                 St Réal Chambéry ⎭   Grenoble to Chambéry
                 search for the cave?
                 at that point the body could be found
                 packaging the corpse
                 (dressed in paramilitary uniform etc. . . .)
                 everything suggests a revenge by the organisation
                 search for former maquis members
As the investigation progresses
it uncovers elements of story 1
e.g.   hot country
       cold country
       Consul
       school friends?
A whole sequence of clues
                 15 May, "Un R est un M," etc. (invent lots of
                 etc.)
                 have a single purpose, to establish a relation
                       53D → Grenoble Chambéry Maquis
                 Chartreuse

a different sequence should
      lead towards "truth" = treason

f°7

1   Serval disappearance
2   First dues produce nothing   3 the hot country   4 the cold
                                                          country
5   "Un R est un M qui se P le L de la R"
6   Stendhal and Saint-Réal; between Grenoble and Chambéry;
        the Chartreuse, *The Red and the Black*
7   The Chartreuse affair, 1
8   In search of witnesses
9   The Consul
10 X
11 The island, the cave, discovery of the corpse
12 The revenge of the organisation (maquis)
13 explanation

f° *8*

In the absence
of any concrete lead
the "investigation" can only use
the diary notes (coded as far as Lise and the addresses are
        concerned)
        the draft
        the incomplete manuscript (*The Crypt*)   G Postoff
        the detective novel
        (*The Magistrate is the Murderer*)   Grace Hillof

Which is why Xavier is called in
even   *precisely   allumettes*
                        allummetts

"The translation"

The black hand
end 1

f⁰ 9

the mirror of the bishop (of Agde)
the bishop practises blessings
(Stendhal, *The Red and the Black*)

Serval's notes:
petits faits vrais
stretched by the
requirement to imitate
R M P L C
"Un C de P au M d'un C"

f⁰ 10

Clues from *La Chartreuse de Parme*
(or from *The Red and the Black*)

What's at stake is making Salini find out
    that the affair
took place between Grenoble and Chambéry
    (somewhere along that road),
in the Chartreuse massif.

therefore clues
    which make reference
        to names

The only thing that's clear from the start
is that the novels have nothing in common with each other
apart from the fact that Serval is also the name of a central
character in *53 Days*.
Even if Serval had the book in front of him
it would mean nothing
he has nothing to do with
    a hot country or a cold one,
    has never murdered a consul.

f° II

What do you know when you've read the novel to the end? Nothing, except that for quite unknown reasons Serval has been given the manuscript of a detective story one of whose protagonists (the one you think is the victim until he is finally unmasked as the culprit) has the same name as he does. You can see straight away that this single clue has a deeper meaning: that Serval, who is believed to be innocent, is in fact guilty, and that the person or persons who murdered him did so by means and for reasons which are given somewhere in the book. The truth is in the book, is encrypted in it, in exactly the same way that the investigation which culminates in the incrimination of the unwitting narrator of *53 Days* is conducted on the basis of clues provided by the manuscript entitled *The Crypt*.

But when you can see that, you see nothing; the affair might be to do with a woman, or connected with Madame Serval, or with a mistress of Serval's, or it might be related to Serval's business interests, or to his political affairs, or to the part he played in the Resistance.

not a thing

Resistance   Robert Serval alias Bérot
53 D   alias Serval
    Stéphane Réal   Robert

f° 12

This snow-covered waste ground is like an immense blank page where the people we are seeking have inscribed not only their movements and gait, but their secret thoughts too . . .
                    Gaboriau
                    Monsieur Lecoq (1868)

see also "The Beryl Coronet" by Conan Doyle
    in *Adventures of Sherlock Holmes*

a book entitled "The Salzburg Branch"

f° 13

6 weeks

Serval
knows from Lise that the Consul is leaving for 2 months
that the narrator should go back to France for the school holidays
that the Consul knows the narrator
      he hired him for the French Book Exhibition
he researches the narrator learns he was at school at Etampes
pretends to be a former classmate
during a dinner between Serval, the Consul, and Lise, the question of the narrator's gifts as a detective is raised
▷ Serval hints for the 1st time that he is threatened
▷ Serval asks the Consul to protect him
      knowing that the Consul is leaving Grianta
▷ so asks for Narrator's address and telephone number

– Disappears
– Recovers his car

Circumstances of disappearance
in context of State of emergency

Very stringent controls at the
port, airport, stations, etc.
<u>so</u>   has not left
<u>so</u>   has been killed

Intervention of the French | Embassy | WHERE IS HE REALLY

---

disappears before declaration of state of emergency?

15 January: the Consul engages the narrator
18   Lise and Serval   <u>dead line:</u> 15 May
      decide that the fall   date of Consul's departure for
      guy will be the   France
      wee teacher

February	Serval investigates the narrator
March ⎫ April ⎭	Serval writes "The Crypt" which will provide the Narrator with the false clues
May 1	Serval tells the Consul that he is threatened
May 3	Serval tells the Consul that he knows the Narrator
May 8	State of Emergency (not foreseen: that <u>must</u> get in the way)
May 12	Serval disappears; investigation
May 15	Consul summons Narrator

> OR ELSE: The Consul gives the case to the
> Narrator WITHOUT the Police knowing
> He came to see me and asked me to give you this
> ???

July 1	Consul returns
July 2	Consul murdered at Lise's
July 2, later	the Narrator goes to Lise's finds the corpse
July 3	arrest of Narrator, <u>obviously</u> guilty of the Consul's murder

f° 14

The Marquis, p. 179
   One of the Vercors leaders (Reynies) arrested by Gestapo
   after denunciation by a Frenchman. (His body was never
   found.)

French against the French chapter 7 139 —
Multon (alias Lunel) Bertin's assistant (Bertin being Frenay's
right-hand man) ("Combat" network) (Resistance organisation at
Lyon and Marseille)
is "turned around" by Dunker, the head of the Marseille Gestapo,

and betrays 125 *résistants* in Marseille (5 of whom agree to work for the Gestapo). Then transferred to Lyon with another traitor, Robert Moog, where they work under the control of Klaus Barbie. supposed to watch a "letter box" in Rue Bouteille used by the "Rail-Sabotage" group whose leader is called (codename) Didot (René Hardy) (the group is responsible for many derailments)

> Lecussan head of the Lyon
> paramilitary police
> Dehau
> Filliol
> Boynichon (?)
> Chambéry: Touvier
> (afterwards at Lyon)

2. Sheets not filed

f⁰ 1

53 Days functions
as a <u>model</u>
for Salini

ch 1   the narrator has a mission entrusted to him
        Etampes
ch 2   reading *The Crypt*
ch 3   search for all the relations
        between *The Crypt* and the life,
        known or hidden, of
        Réal-Serval

similarly

ch 14   Salini has the investigation
        entrusted to him
ch 15   what is known about it (as good as nothing)
ch 16   search for all the
        relations between *53 Days* and
        the life, known or hidden, of Serval-Louviers

                    S R V L-L V R S
                    E   A   OU IE
                    R   L
                    VAL   SER
                        di

f⁰ 2

Louviers 1

What is the function of *53 Days*?
To provide an <u>acceptable</u>, <u>plausible</u> explanation of
Serval's disappearance
and to give clues that are
opaque and translucent enough
to allow the <u>body</u> to be found

with the body, the confession of the 2 avengers
which the police and public opinion will
accept all the more easily
as there are no other trails

so the Serval affair is shelved
and Patricia Serval inherits

BUT:
Why not an explicit crime?
Why need the book *53 Days*
What's the point of so much deceptiveness in
the book
if the purpose is for everything to be obvious
once the body is discovered?

> The "explanation" must be given by the
> clues in the *53 Days* book before the body
> is discovered (which will merely <u>confirm</u>
> what the "linguistic" investigation has
> hypothesised)

What happens when Serval receives the novel

f° 3

Louviers 2

Because Serval was a former government official
the DST *[French Intelligence Service]* conducted its own enquiry, in
parallel to the police
It considered: a settling of political scores
       :   an assassination committed by extremists from
            France or more probably from the Third World
            (in particular as a consequence of a deal between
            one of Serval's businesses and Chile or
            Argentina)

The official investigation is directed towards
        :   kidnapping with ransom demand
        :   crime of passion (Patricia Serval is suspected)
        :
        :

IN FACT   : Who killed Serval   The "Consul" cannot be a
           and how   comrade in arms or a close
                              friend of Robert Serval
Hired hands?   because the naughts and
hard to think up   crosses story on page 21
anything else [? . . .]   would be too obvious
rather: Patricia Serval's lover ("the Consul")
bullet in the neck
then puts him into a German officer's uniform
how does "the Consul" lure Serval
Serval, innocent or not in the maquis affair, is not going to
let himself get taken to the cave

f° 4

THE PROBLEM OF THE ESSENTIAL CLUE
CHAP 7

The Consul returns to France to "settle his position" id est
to divorce so he can then marry Lise
The Ambassador, who knows, has demanded it
Of course, Serval and Lise know
but nobody else
What is going to do for the Narrator: – the fact that he has been
seen several times in the
company of Lise (Motive)
– gets to the Consul's in the
middle of the night
+ shot(Opportunity)
all witnessed (taxi driver)
– BUT: must have his
it could be:gun shop,antique dealer's   fingerprints on the gun
parcel in the post   (PROOF)
shooting lesson   – he has a gun it's stolen
why has he got a gun
one trail leads towards the shooting master: to have a pretext for
questioning him he asks for a lesson (too flimsy)
Lise should not be a suspect at that point. So must not intervene
(for the reader)

f⁰ s

53 Days: the narrator is
declared guilty of killing
the Consul so as to take his
mistress Lise: these are the
<u>real</u> motives of Serval's plot
(they are not far from being
those of the Narrator, who is madly in love
with Lise. But that's something Serval and
Lise could not predict with certainty. Otherwise they would
<u>really</u> have had the Consul murdered by Lise

The truth, barely touched upon, recedes into the distance.
It has to be sought far beyond any
direct allusion.

FIVE NOTES ON THE TEXT

Page 33, line 21: between "going out" and "together," in a sentence full of vs, the typescript has "(vvvvvvv!)," which suggests that Georges Perec did not consider this to be the final version.

Page 40, Hartz and Hertz: see "Notes on the Drafted Chapters," p. 176 above

Page 49, *Lasciatto*: see "Notes on the Drafted Chapters," p. 177 above.

Page 52, *schlemm*: see "Notes on the Drafted Chapters," p. 177 above, "*chlemm*."

The footnotes on pp. 84 and 85 are Georges Perec's.

HM, JR

FIVE NOTES ON THE
TRANSLATION

The French editors used square brackets to indicate the letters that Perec omitted when abbreviating words and phrases in his handwritten notes and drafts. I have omitted the brackets and thereby made it seem that Perec wrote out in full even his most rapid thoughts for *"53Days."* He did not. For example, the sentence on p. 146 above:

> The Consul entrusts to X an examination of the suitcase found in the boot of Serval's abandoned car.

is the product of transcription, expansion, and translation of:

> *Le Consul charge X d'étudier la valise tvée d le coffre de la voit ab de Serval*

Square brackets in this edition indicate my own additions and explanations.

Perec did not consistently underline the titles of books and films in his handwritten notes. Unlike the editors of the French text, I have tried to standardise the presentation of titles.

The footnotes on pp. 113, 172, and 227 are mine.

I should like to thank Heather Mawhinney, Mathew Hodges and Harry Mathews for their assistance.

DB

About the Author

GEORGES PEREC (1936–1982) was a French novelist, filmmaker, documentalist, and essayist. He was a member of the famed OU-LIPO movement, a loose gathering of writers and mathematicians who seek to create works using constrained writing techniques. Perec's *Life A User's Manual*, has been hailed "one of the great novels of the century" by the *Times Literary Supplement* and the *Boston Globe*.

HARRY MATHEWS and JACQUES ROUBAUD, each a distinguished novelist in his own right, were close friends and collaborators of Georges Perec, as well as fellow members of the OULIPO ("Ouvroir de Littérature Potentielle").

DAVID BELLOS's previous translations of Georges Perec include *Life A User's Manual*, which won the 1988 French American Foundation translation prize, *Things: A Story of the Sixties*, and *W or the Memory of Childhood*. He is also the author of *Georges Perec: A Life in Words* (Godine, 1993), which won the Prix Goncourt for Biography.